Disney

ZOOTOPIA

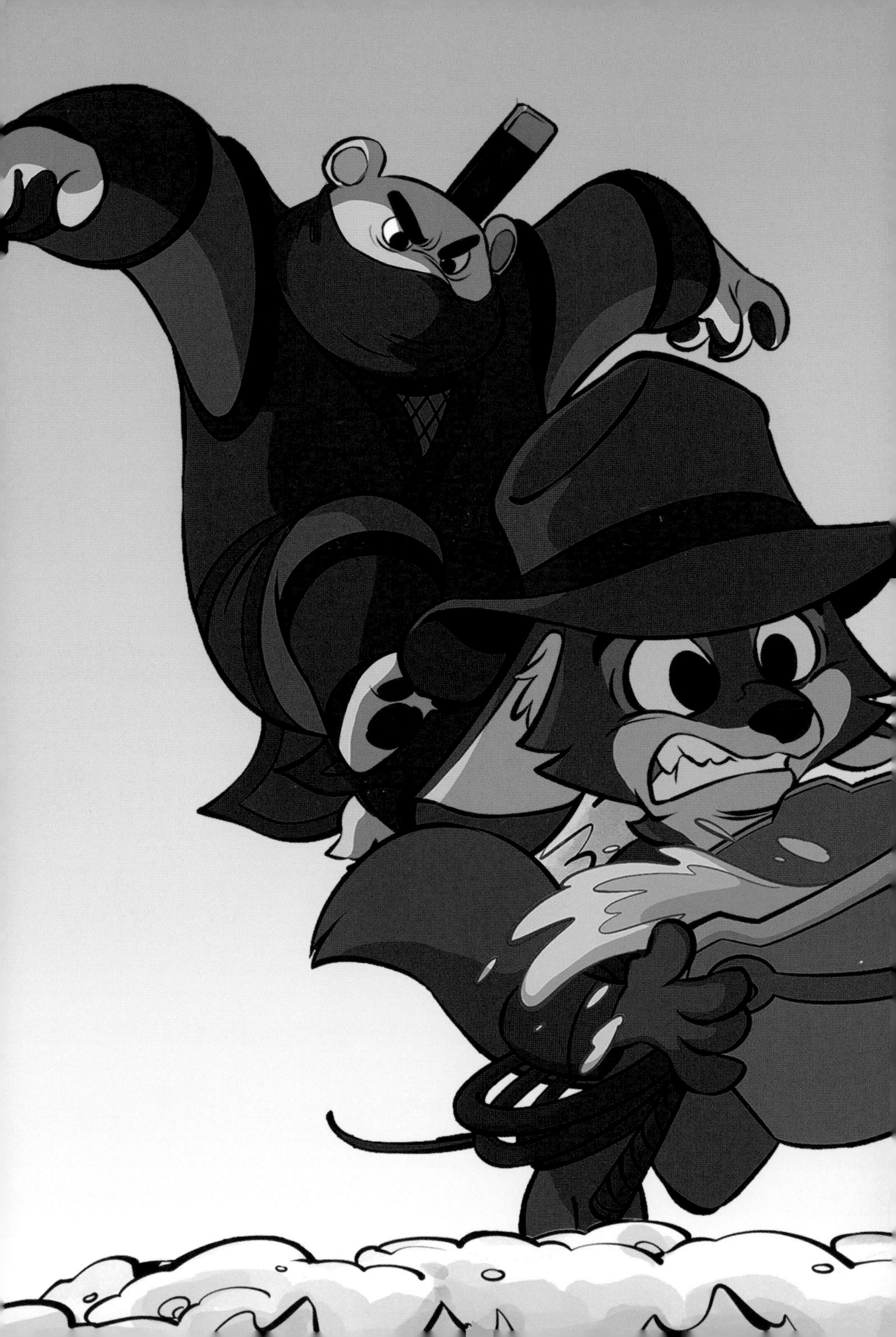

DISNEY ZOOTOPIA

SCHOOL DAYS

Script by
Jimmy Gownley

Art by
Leandro Ricardo da Silva

Colors by
Wes Dzioba

Lettering by
Chris Dickey

Dark Horse Books

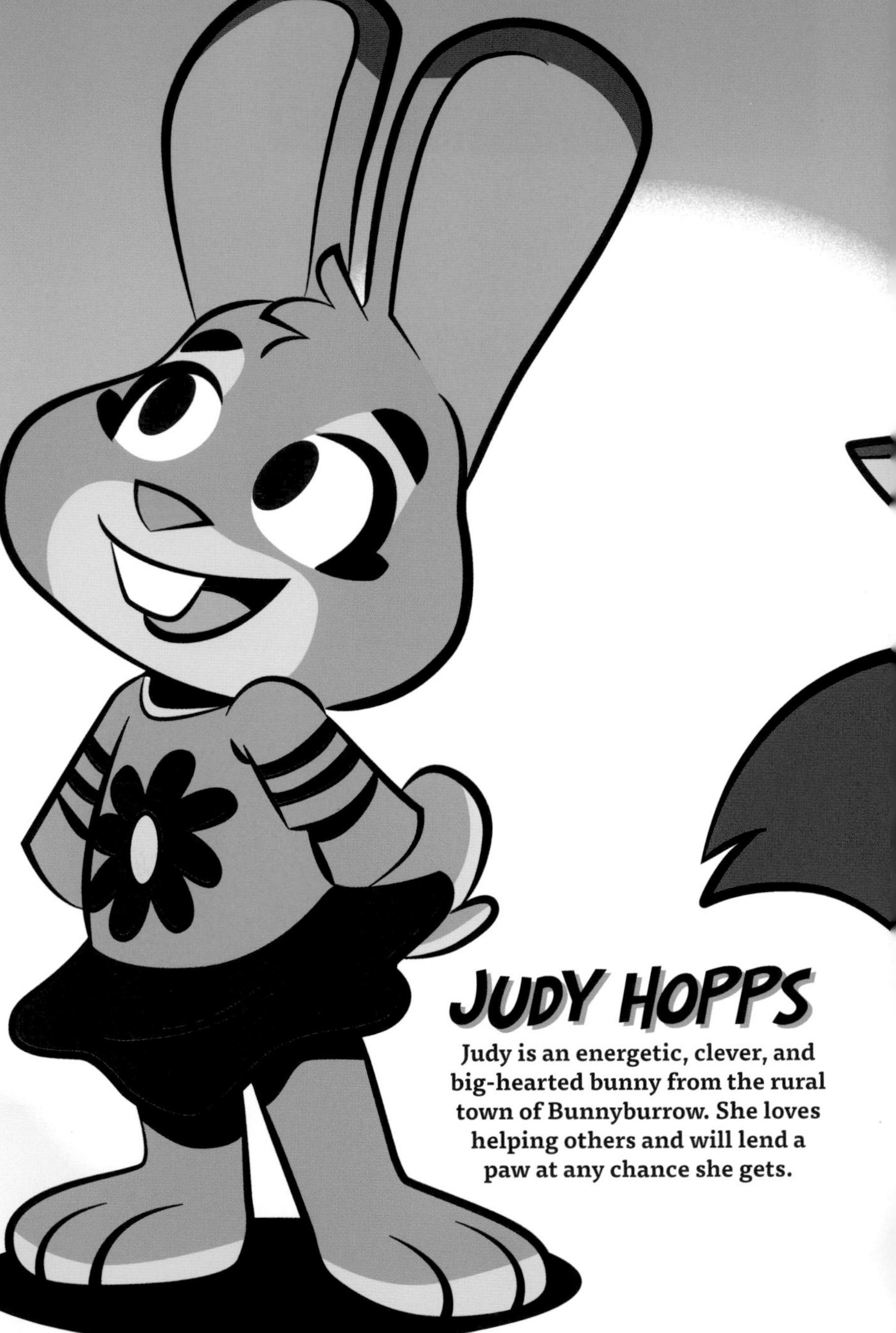

JUDY HOPPS

Judy is an energetic, clever, and big-hearted bunny from the rural town of Bunnyburrow. She loves helping others and will lend a paw at any chance she gets.

NICK WILDE

Nick is a sweet, friendly, and mischievous fox from the big city of Zootopia. He has a natural ability to make others smile and laugh.

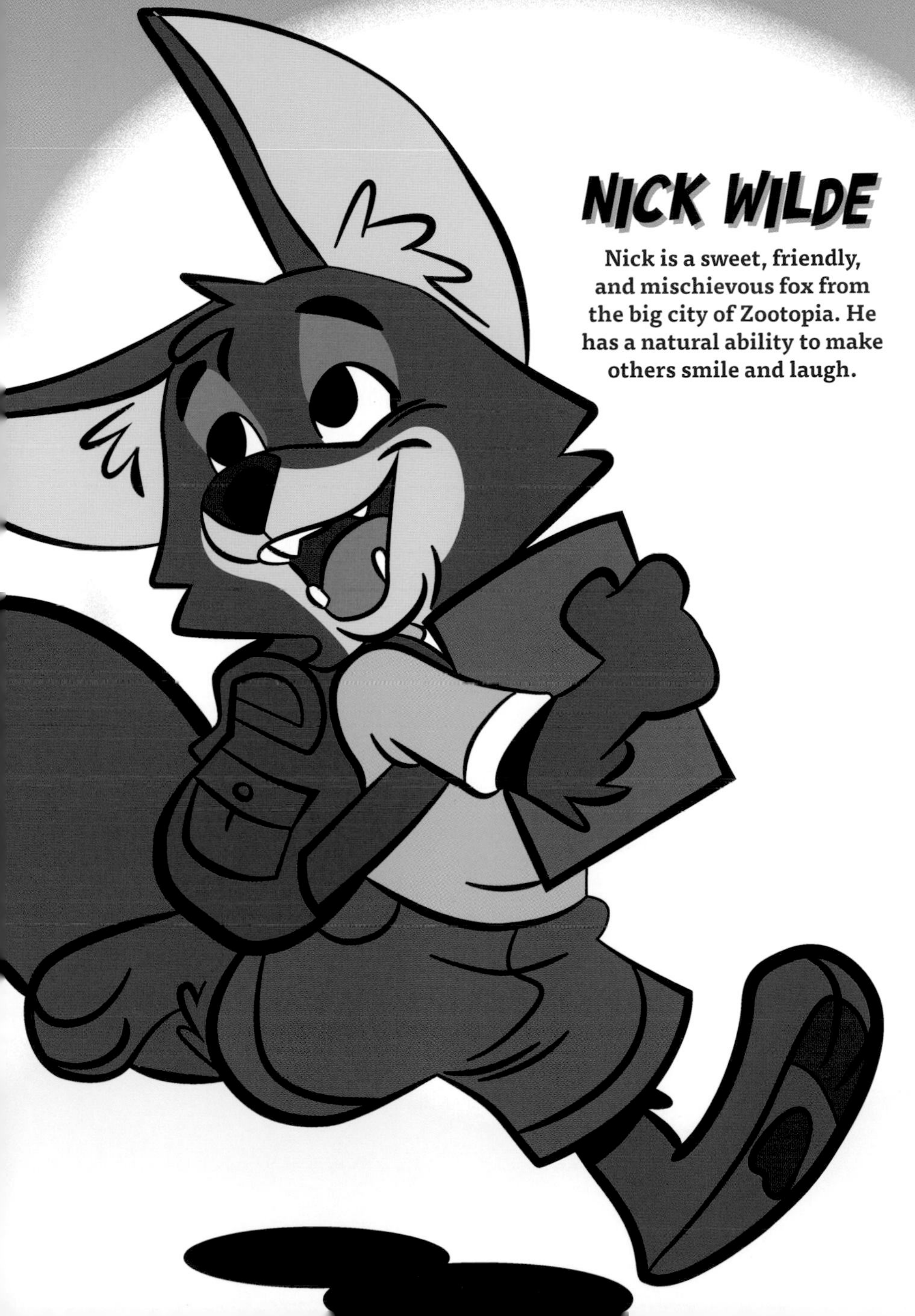

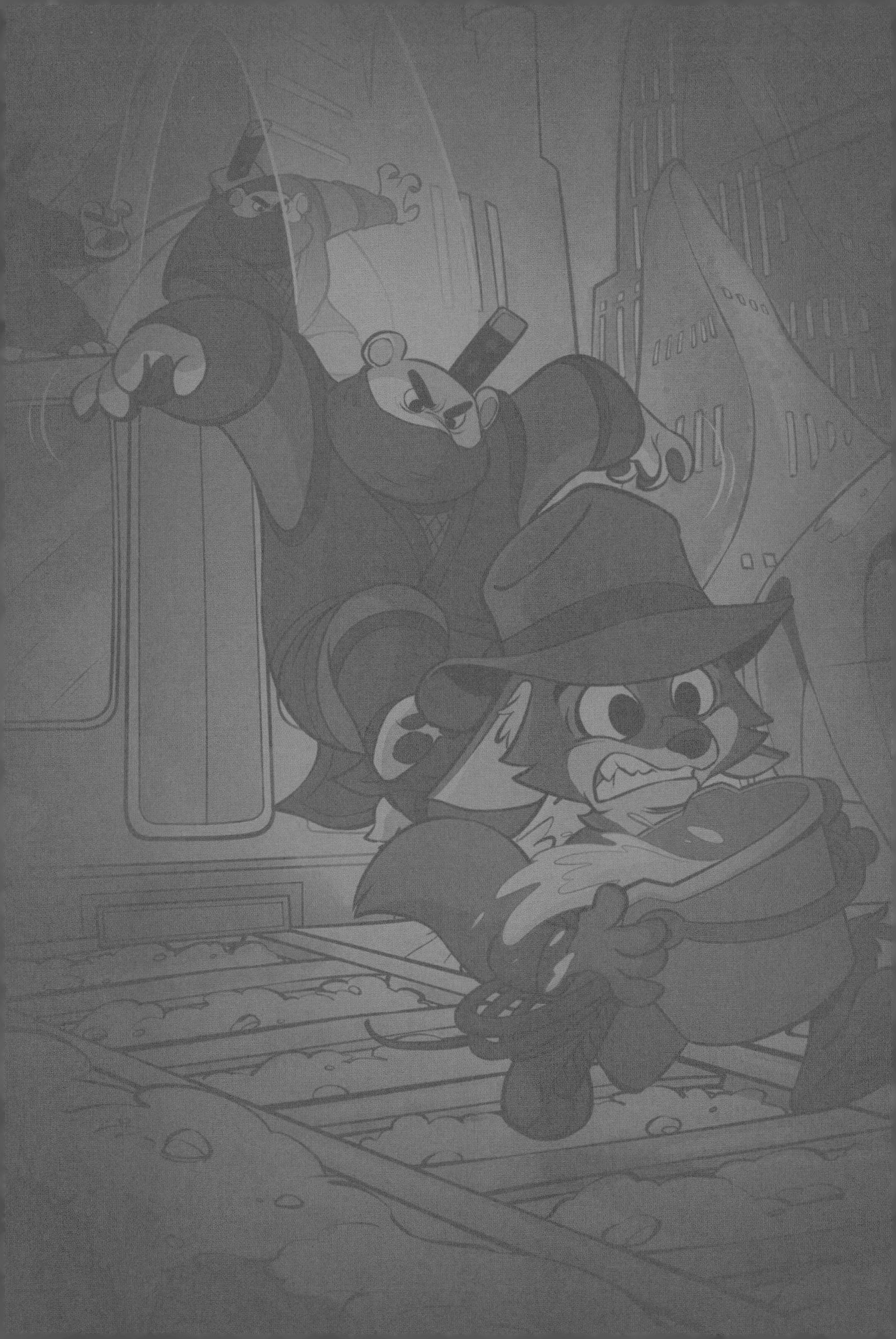

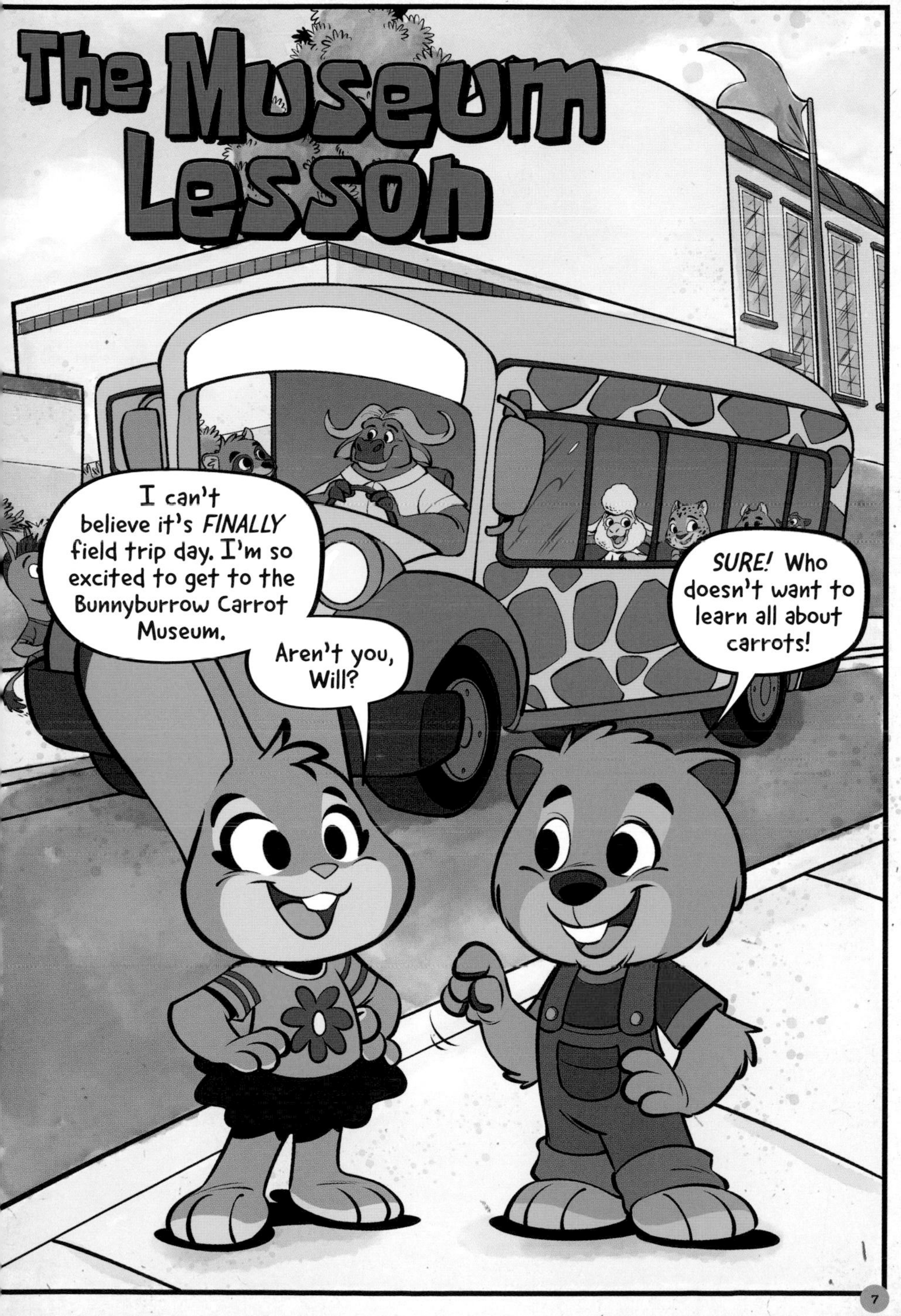
The Museum Lesson
I can't believe it's *FINALLY* field trip day. I'm so excited to get to the Bunnyburrow Carrot Museum.
Aren't you, Will?
SURE! Who doesn't want to learn all about carrots!

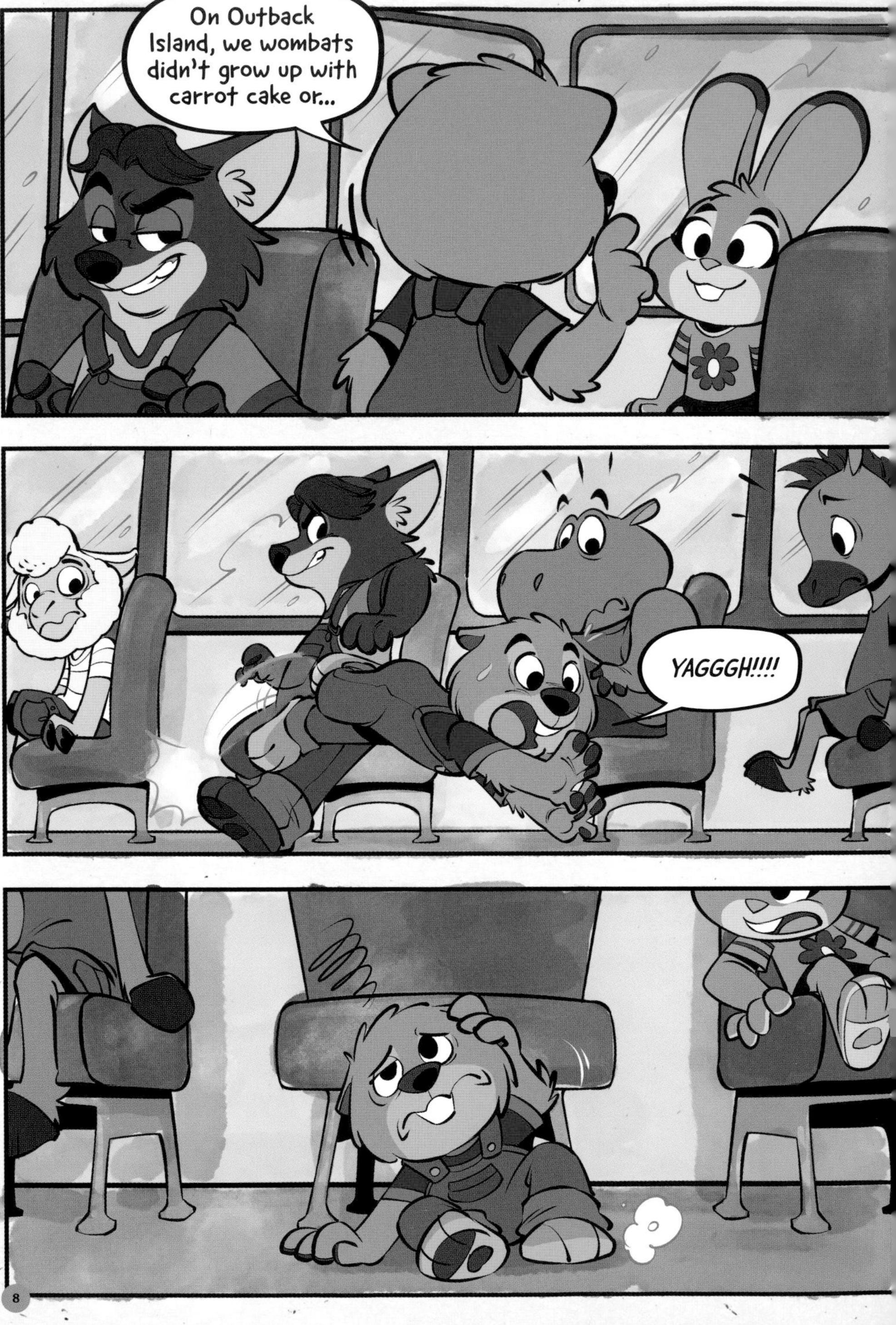
On Outback Island, we wombats didn't grow up with carrot cake or...
YAGGGH!!!!

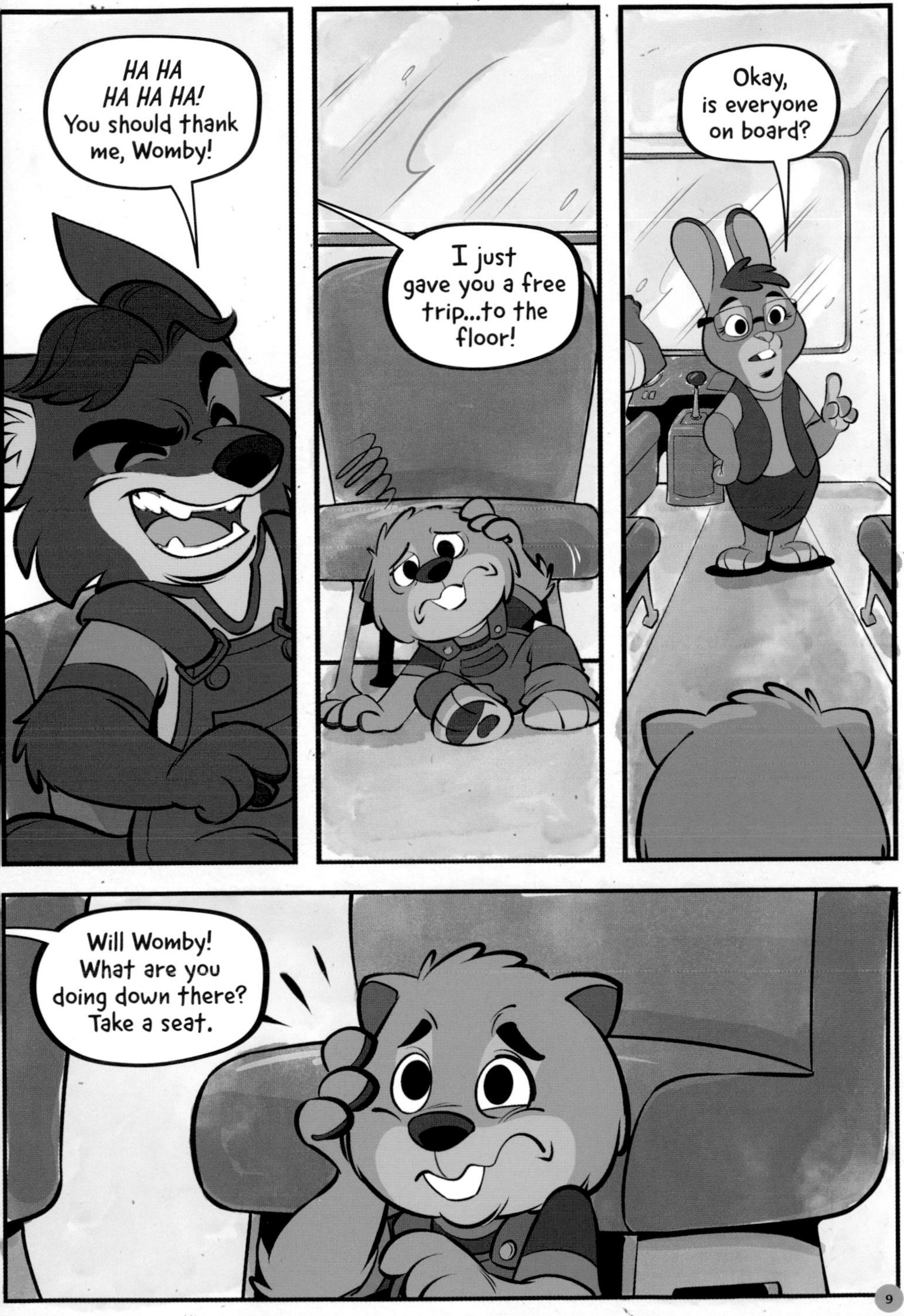
HA HA HA HA HA! You should thank me, Womby!
I just gave you a free trip...to the floor!
Okay, is everyone on board?
Will Womby! What are you doing down there? Take a seat.

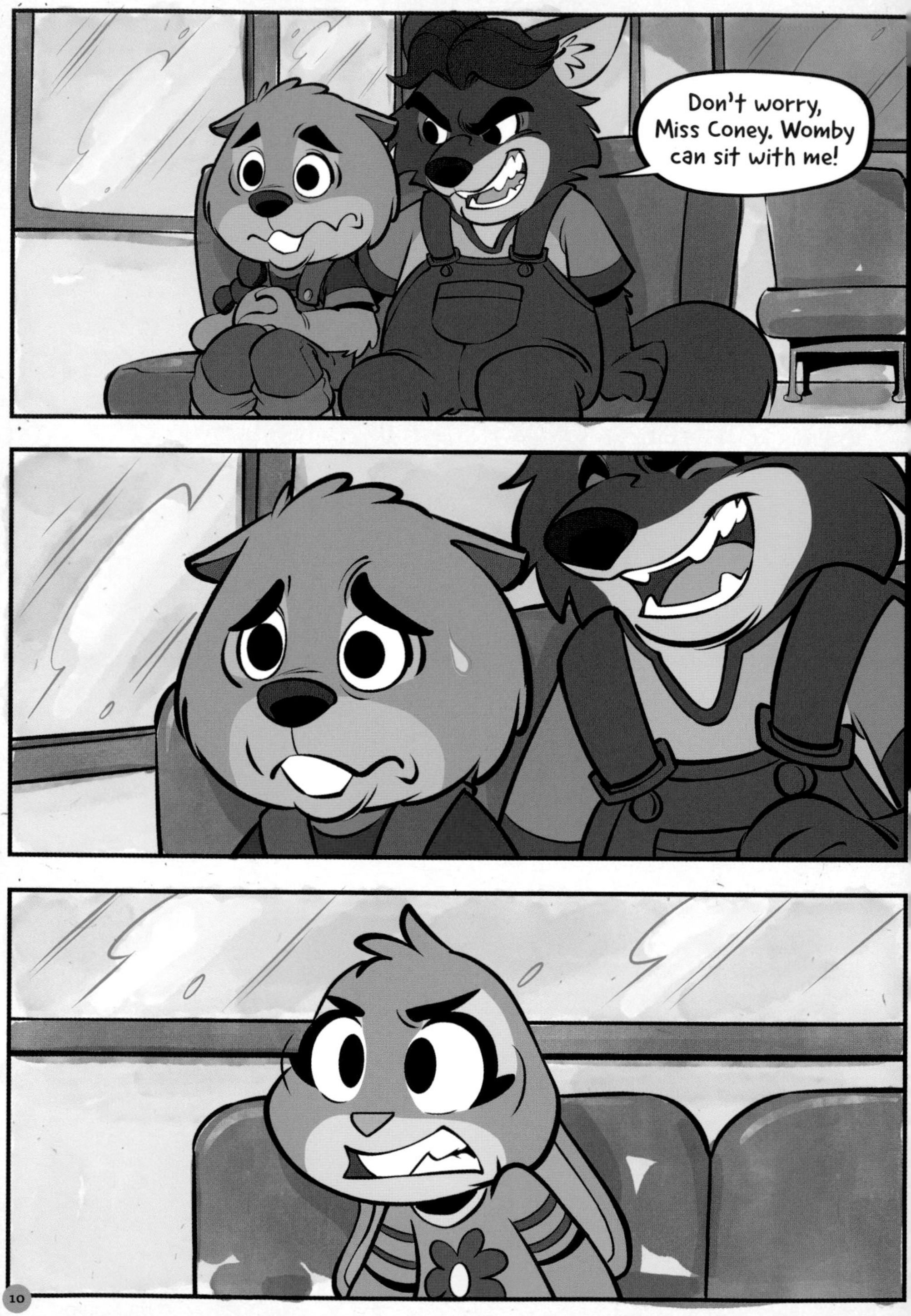
Don't worry, Miss Coney. Womby can sit with me!

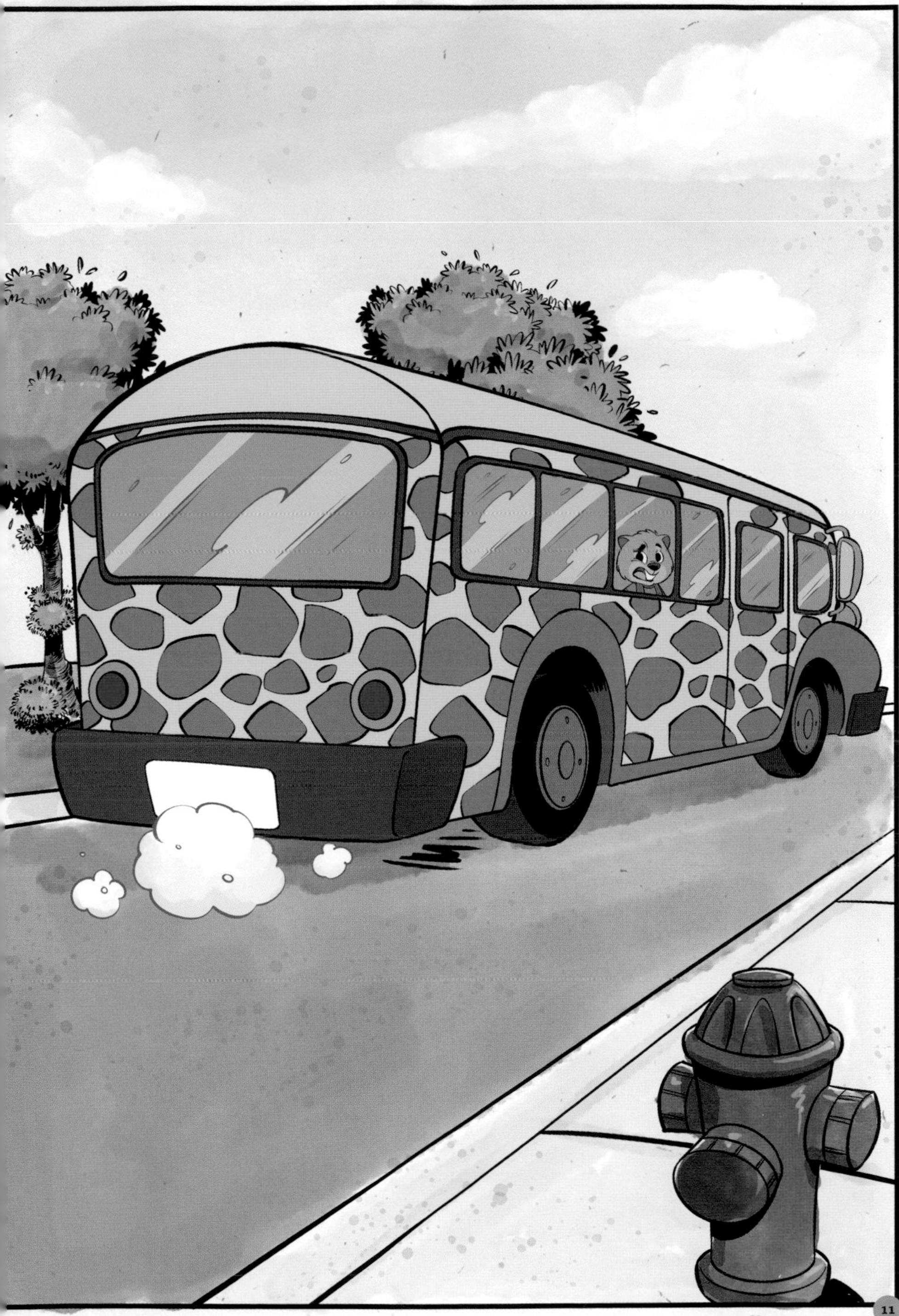

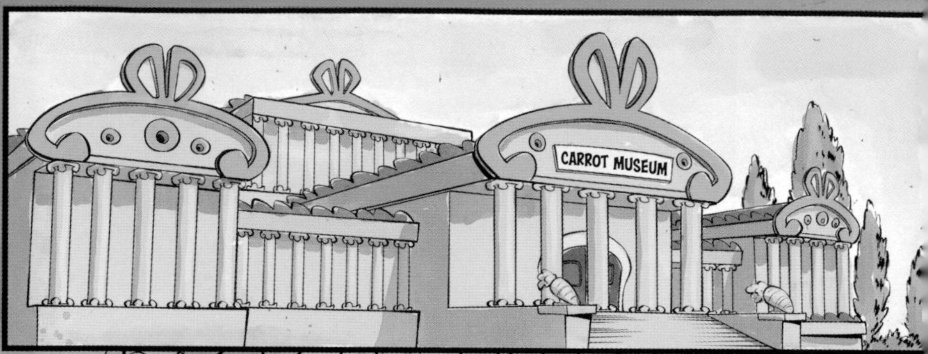
CARROT MUSEUM

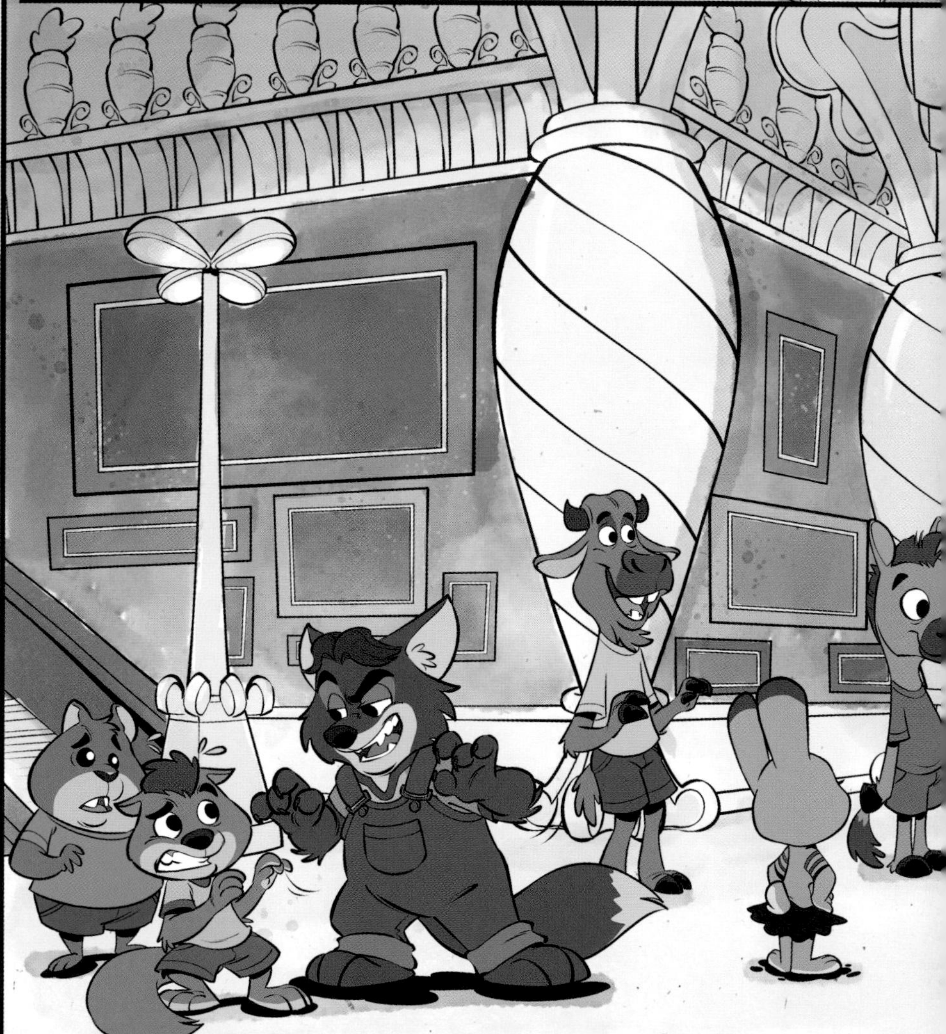

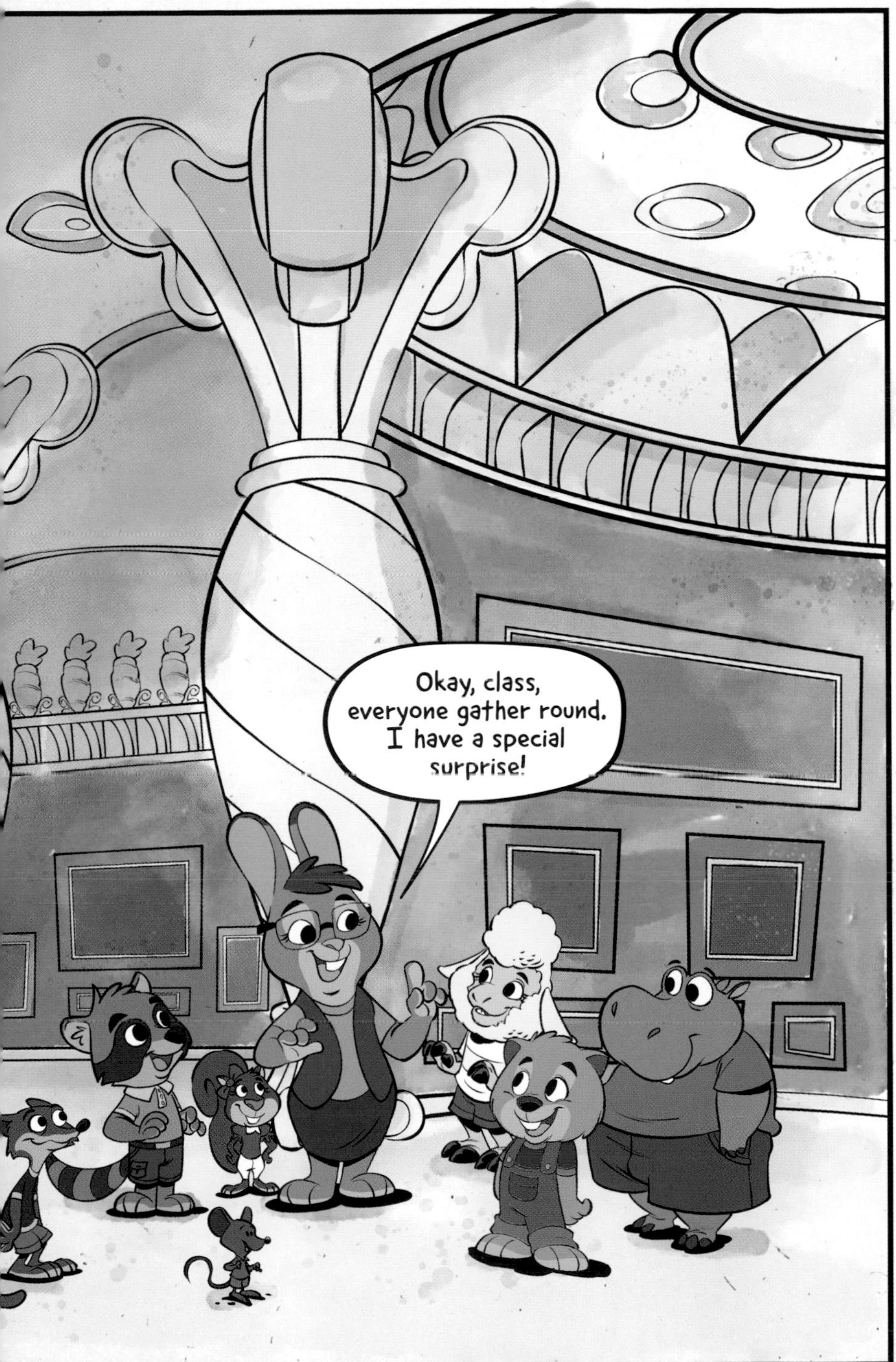
Okay, class, everyone gather round. I have a special surprise!

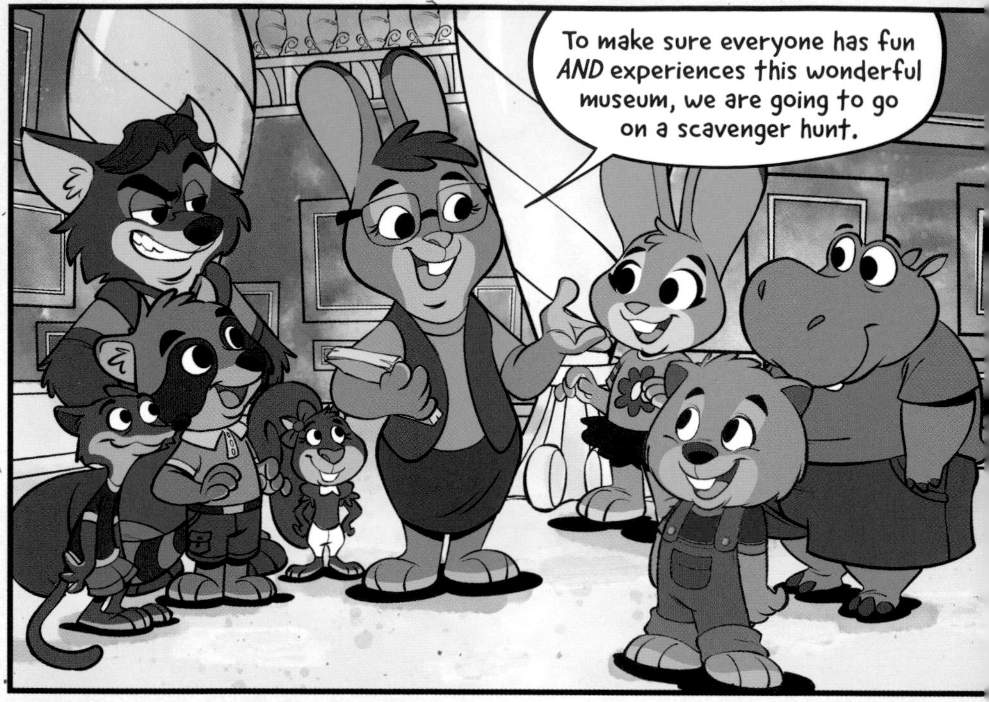
To make sure everyone has fun *AND* experiences this wonderful museum, we are going to go on a scavenger hunt.

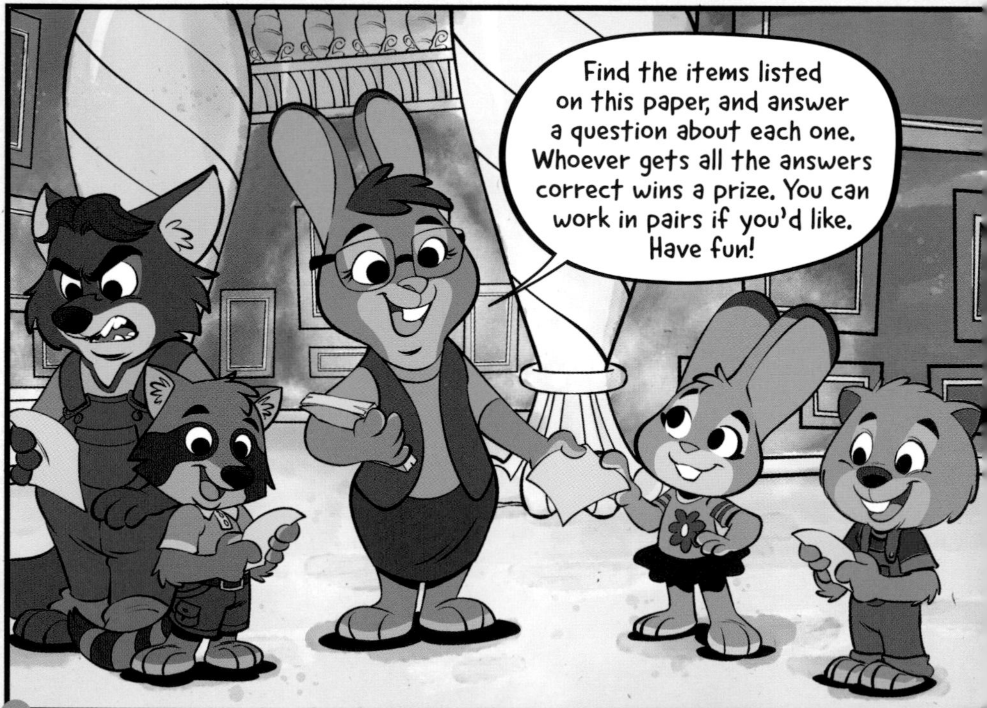
Find the items listed on this paper, and answer a question about each one. Whoever gets all the answers correct wins a prize. You can work in pairs if you'd like. Have fun!

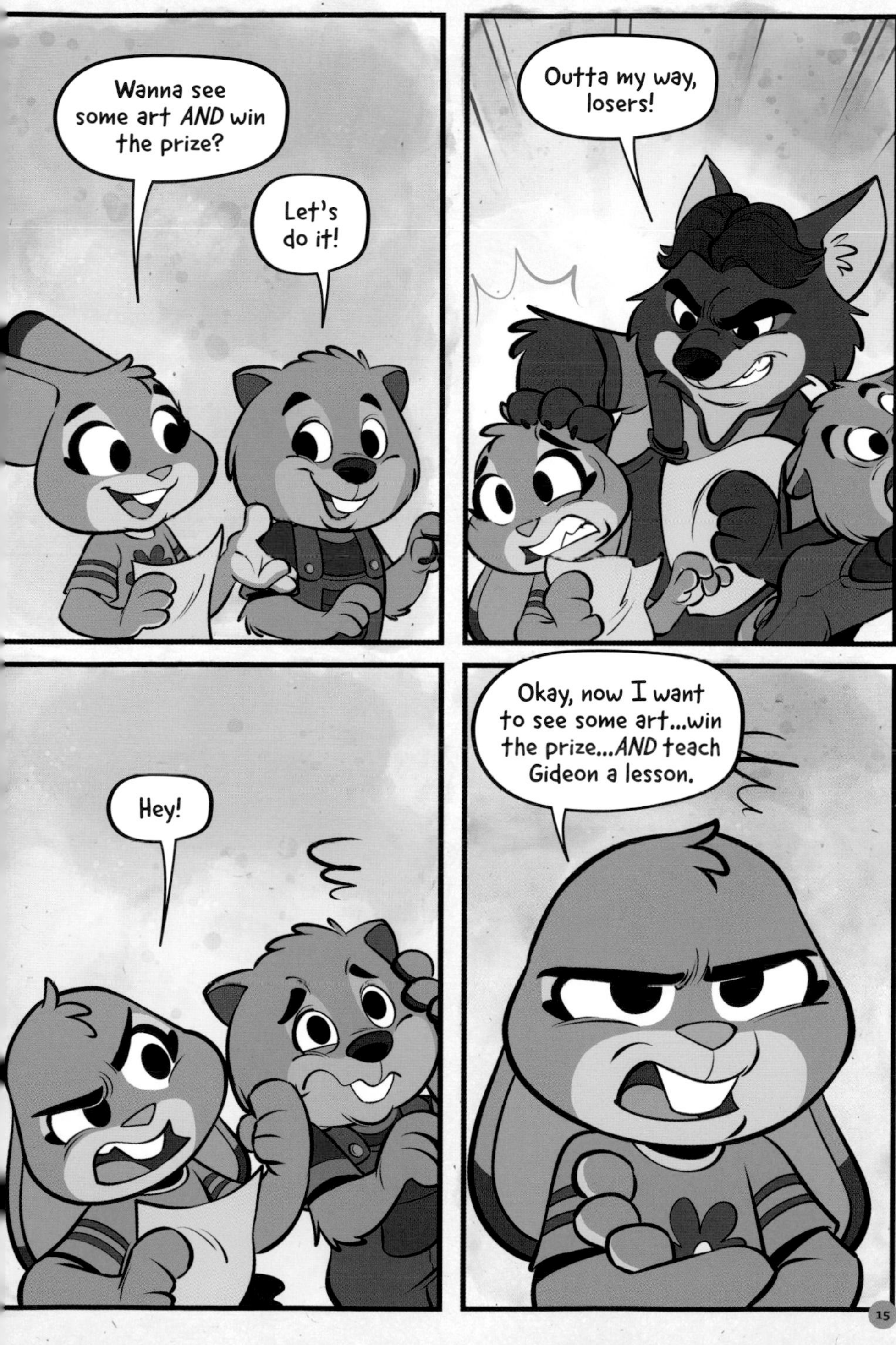
Wanna see some art *AND* win the prize?
Let's do it!
Outta my way, losers!
Hey!
Okay, now I want to see some art...win the prize...*AND* teach Gideon a lesson.

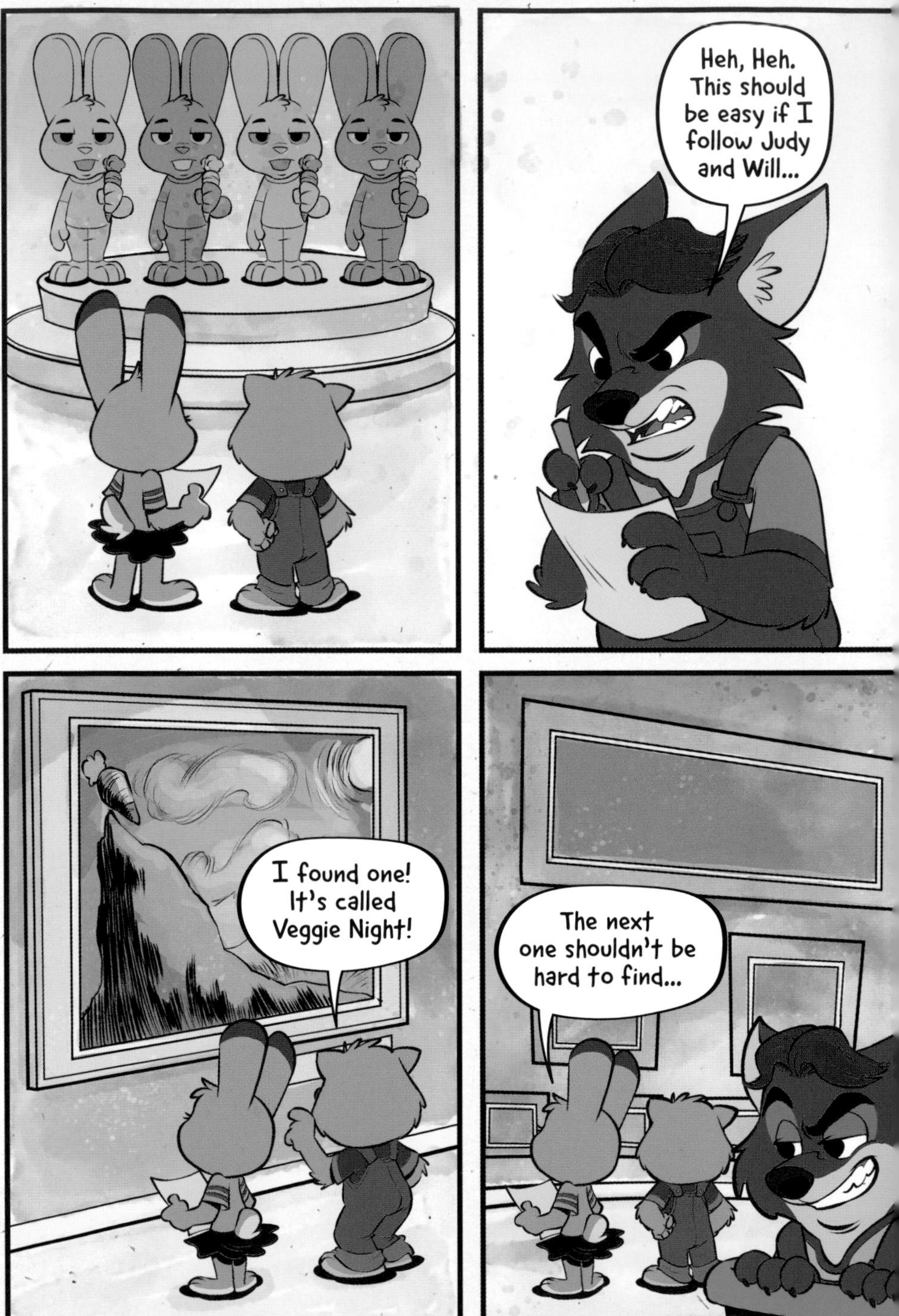
Heh, Heh. This should be easy if I follow Judy and Will...
I found one! It's called Veggie Night!
The next one shouldn't be hard to find...

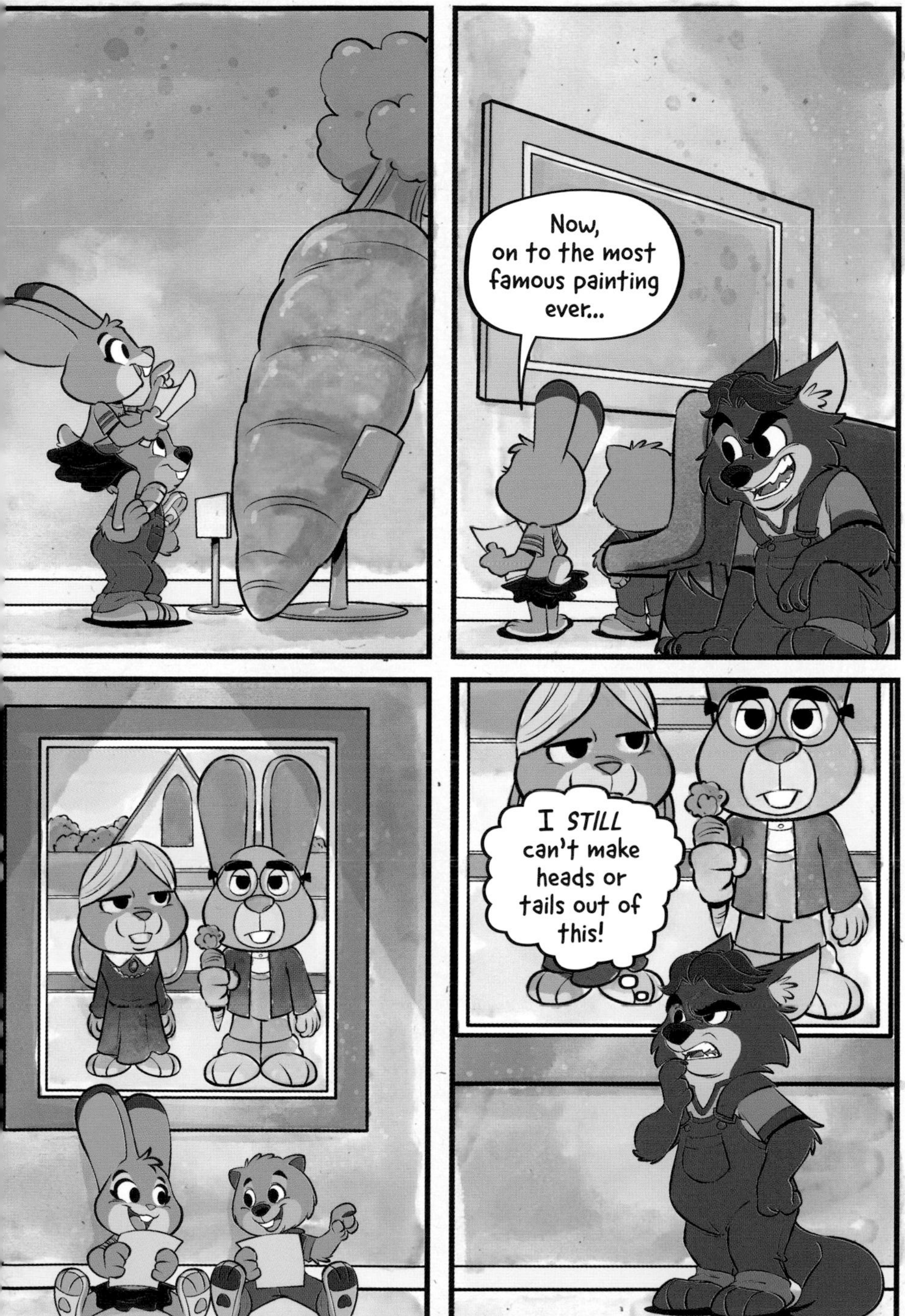
Now, on to the most famous painting ever...
I STILL can't make heads or tails out of this!

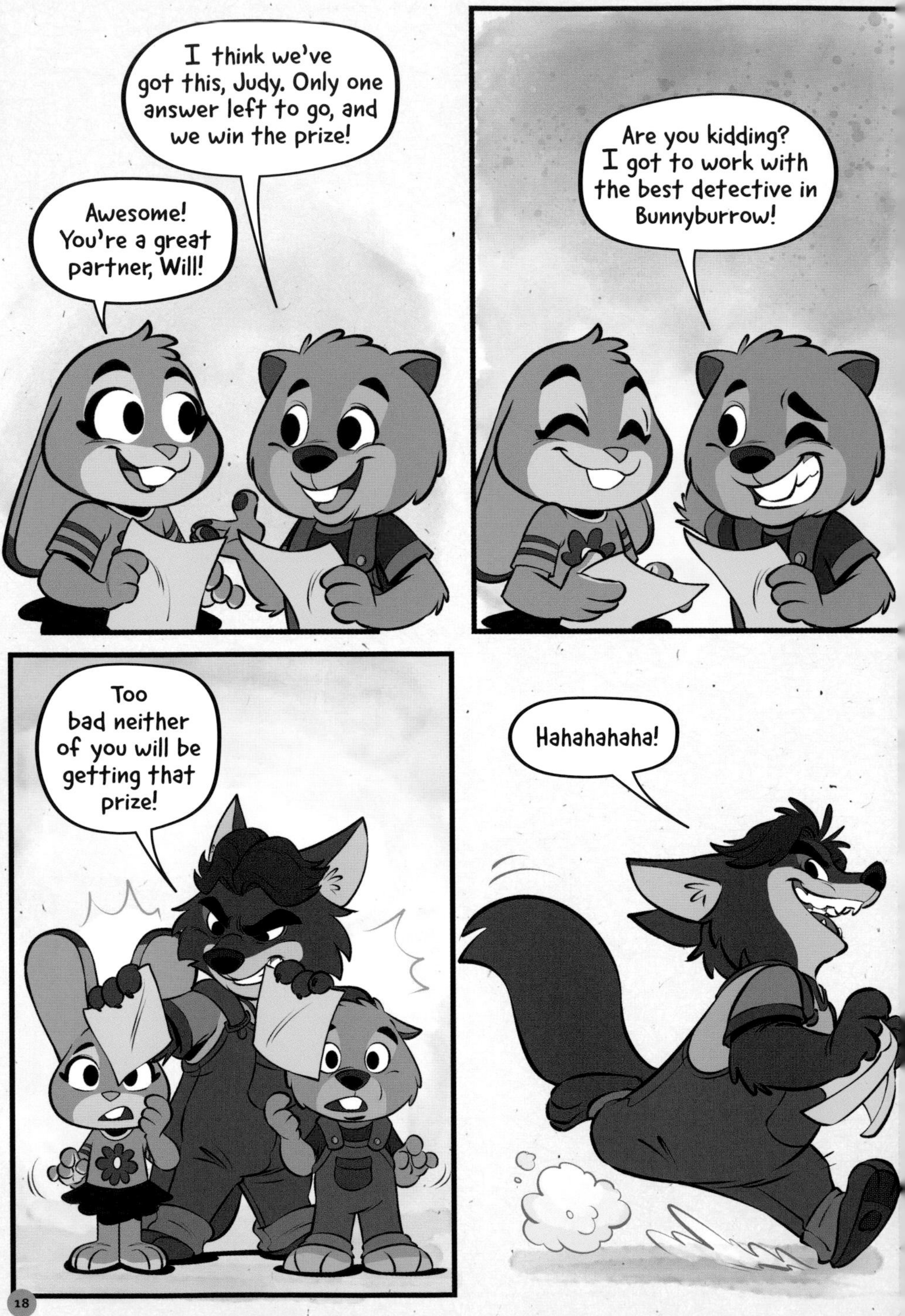
Awesome! You're a great partner, Will!
I think we've got this, Judy. Only one answer left to go, and we win the prize!
Are you kidding? I got to work with the best detective in Bunnyburrow!
Too bad neither of you will be getting that prize!
Hahahahaha!

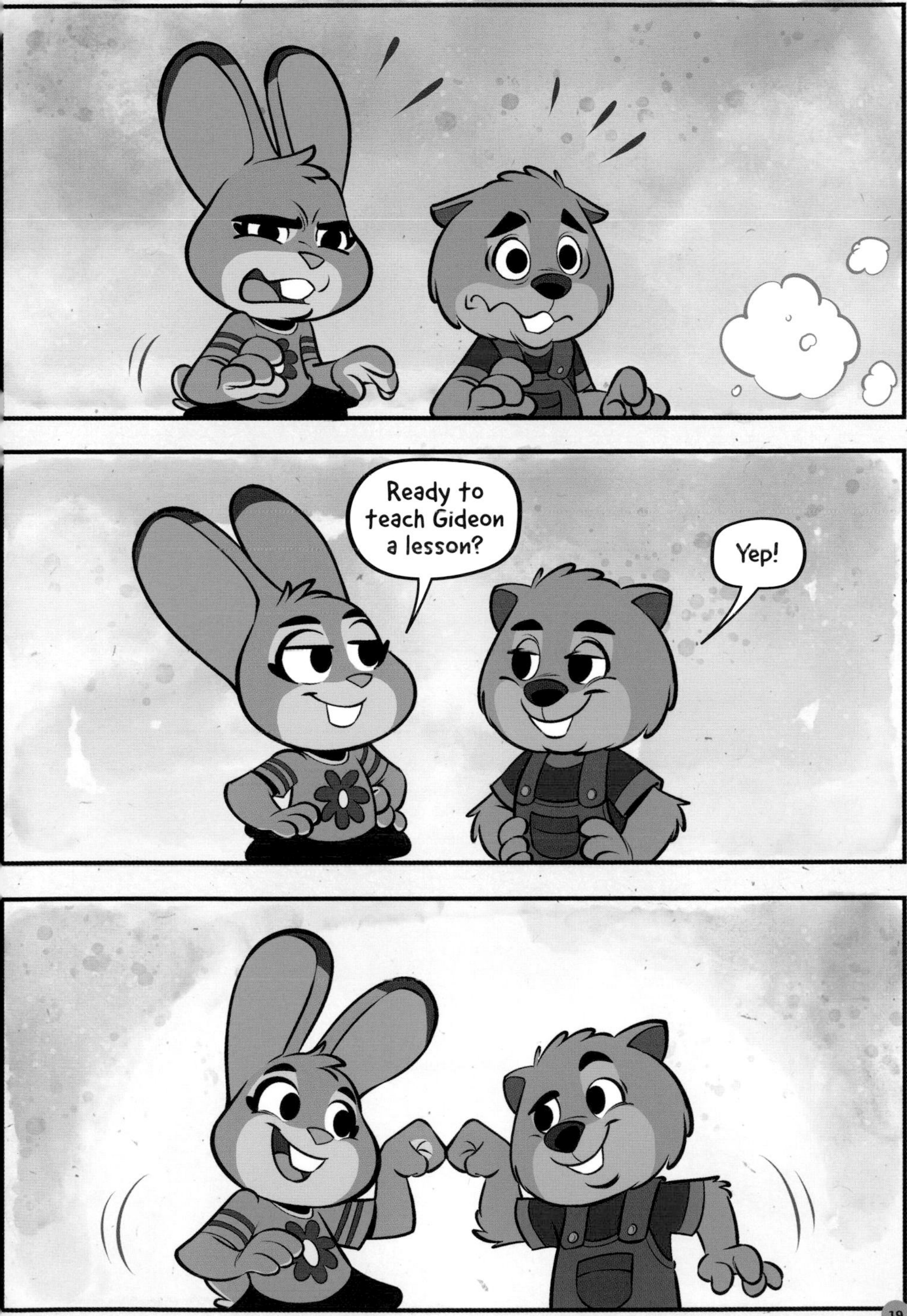
Ready to teach Gideon a lesson?
Yep!

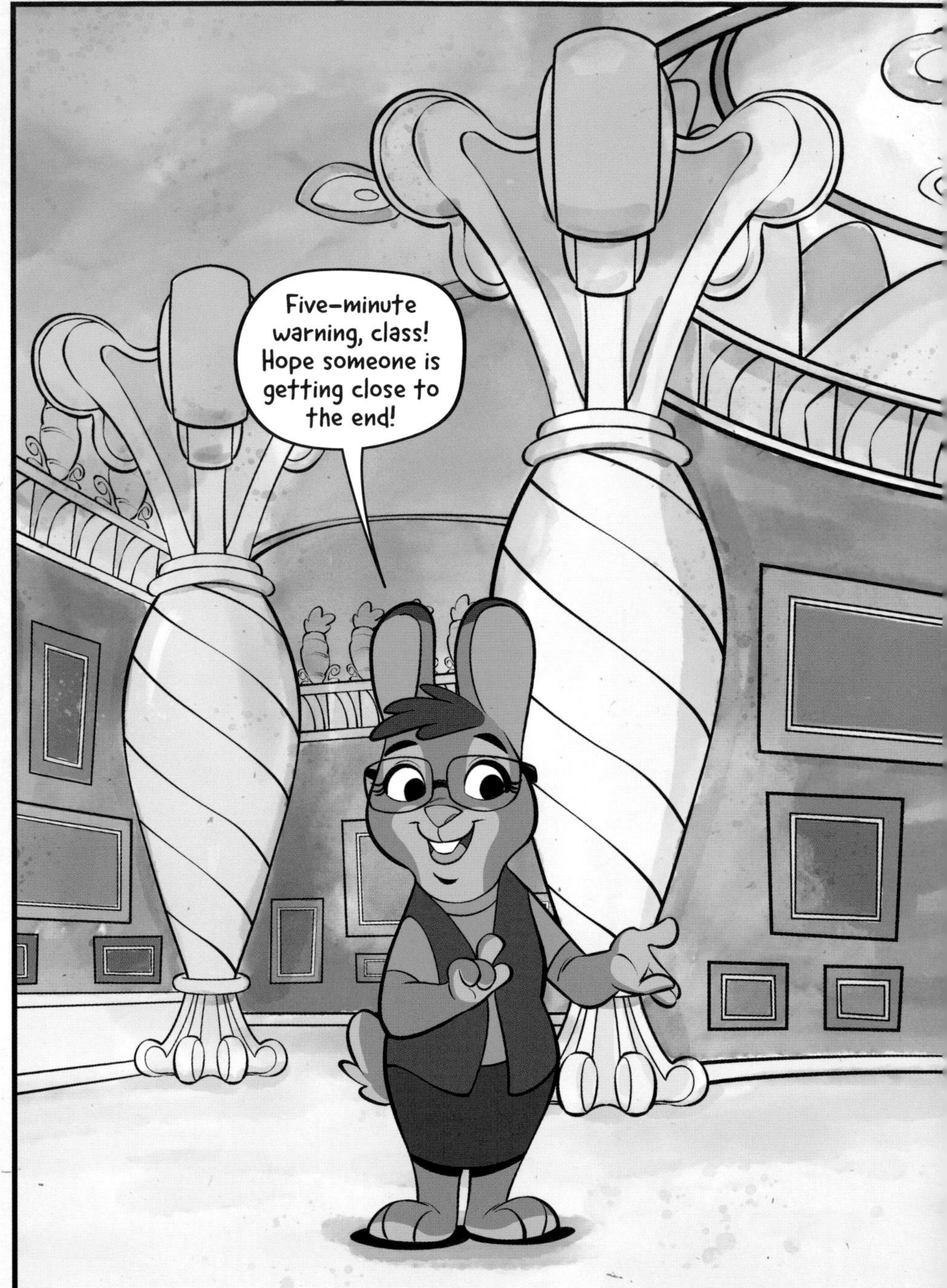
Five-minute warning, class! Hope someone is getting close to the end!

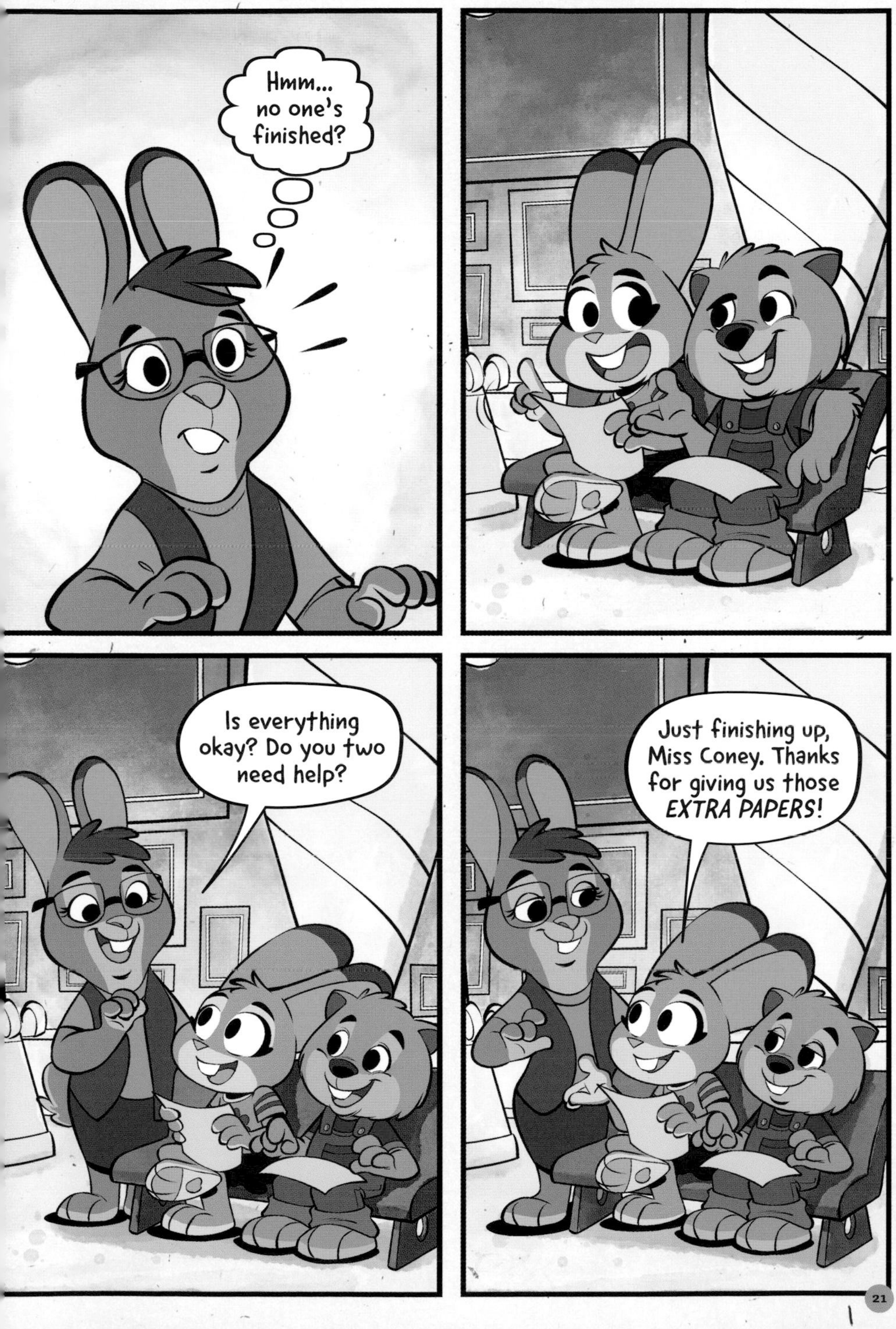
Hmm... no one's finished?
Is everything okay? Do you two need help?
Just finishing up, Miss Coney. Thanks for giving us those EXTRA PAPERS!

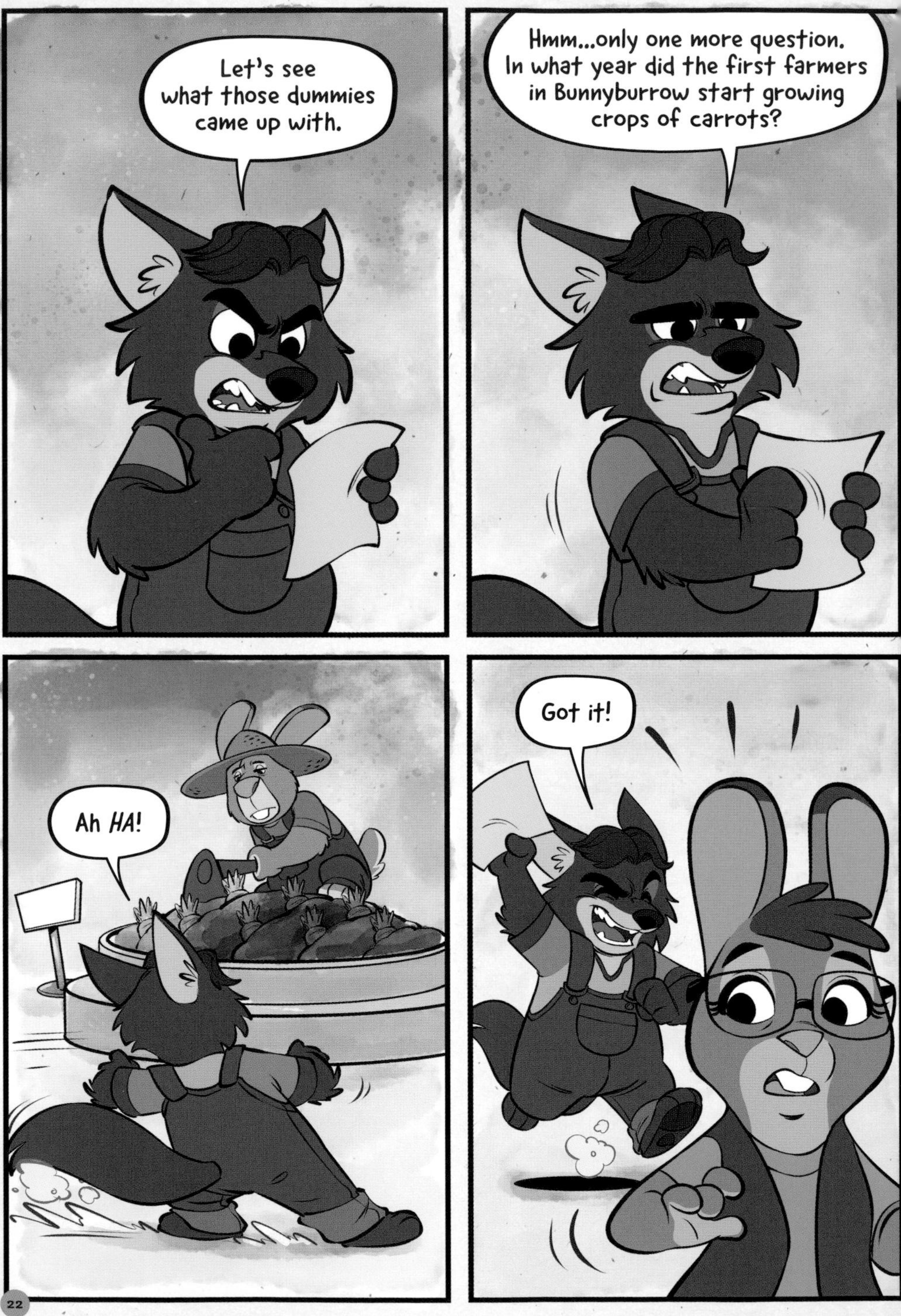
Let's see what those dummies came up with.
Hmm...only one more question. In what year did the first farmers in Bunnyburrow start growing crops of carrots?
Ah HA!
Got it!

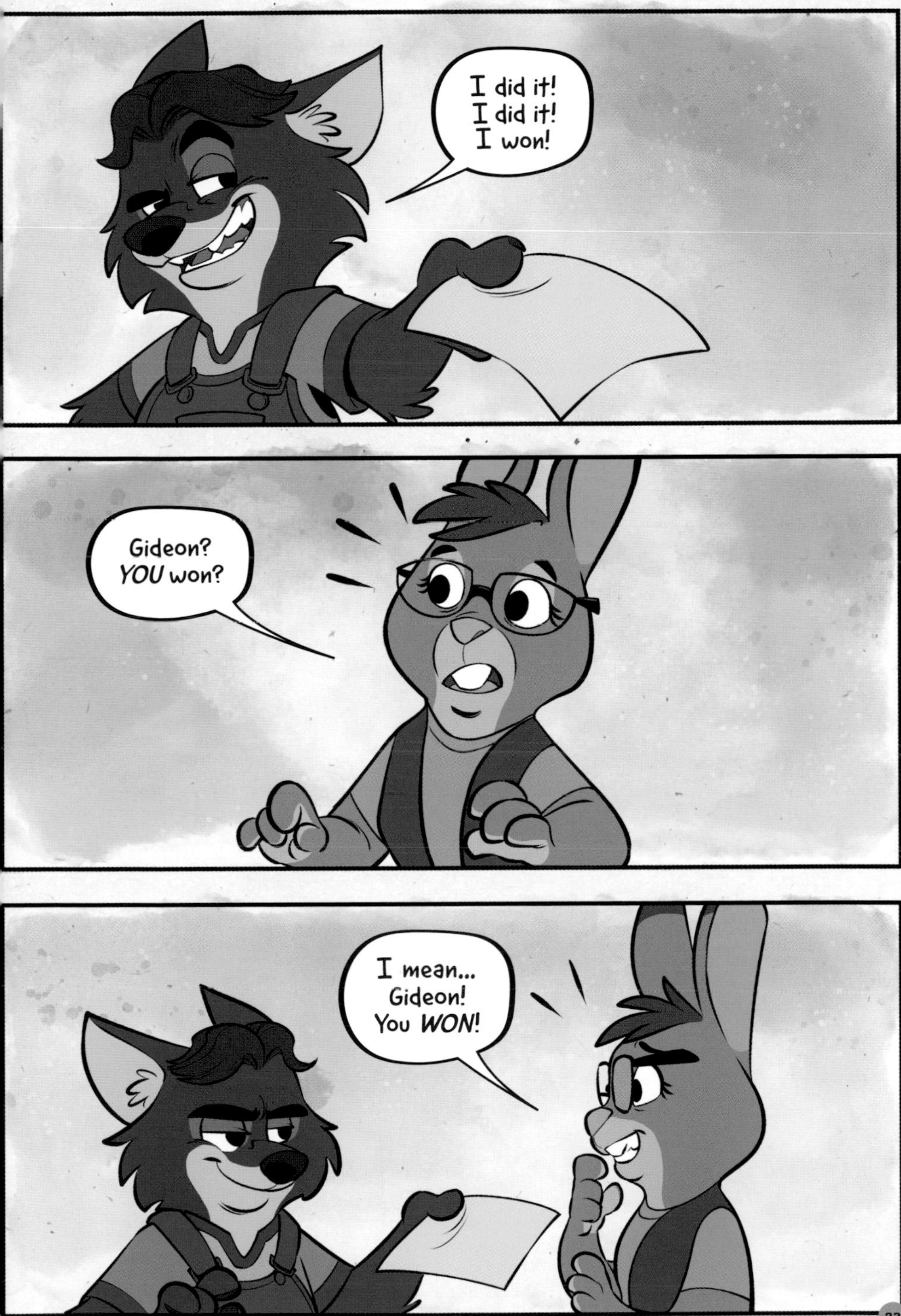
I did it! I did it! I won!
Gideon? *YOU* won?
I mean... Gideon! You *WON*!

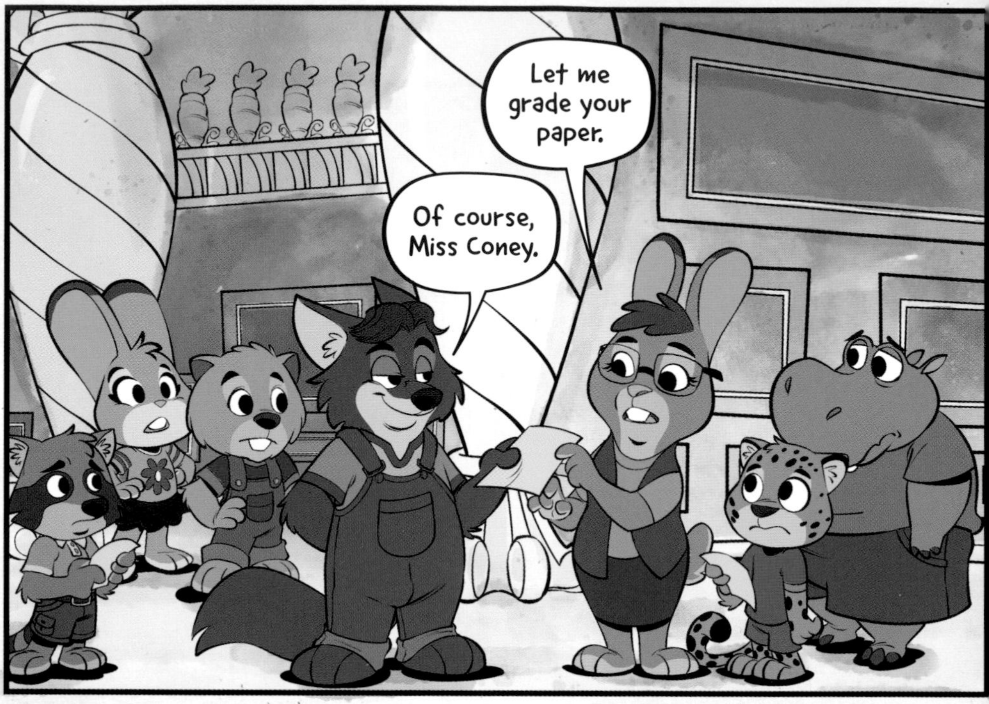
Let me grade your paper.
Of course, Miss Coney.

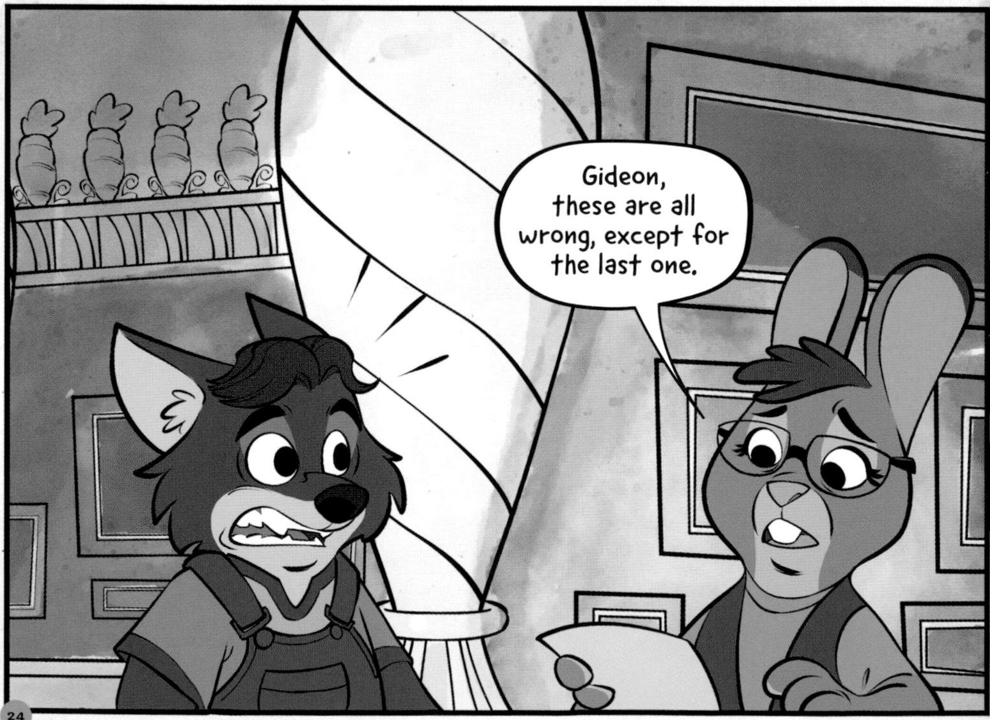
Gideon, these are all wrong, except for the last one.

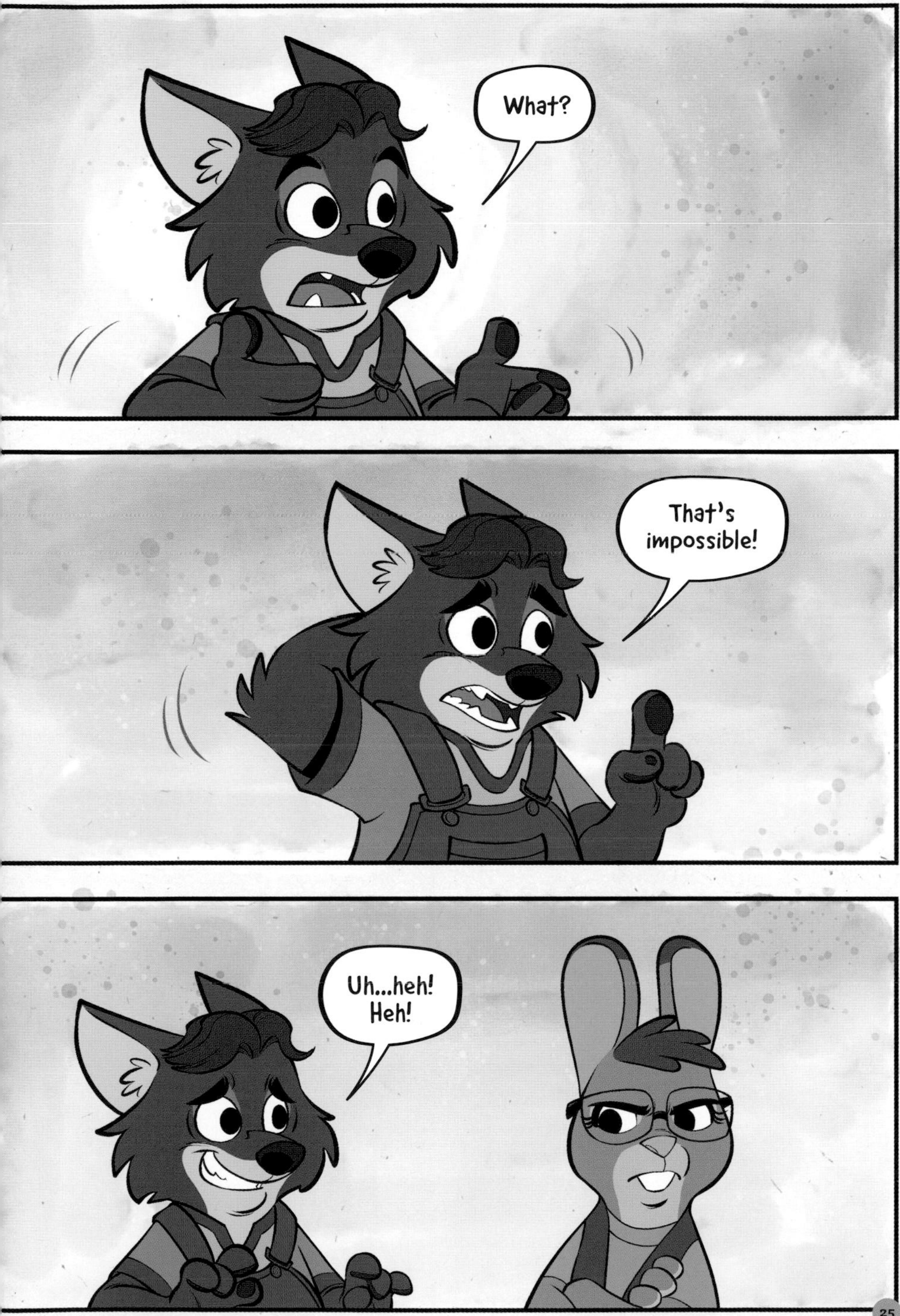
What?
That's impossible!
Uh...heh! Heh!

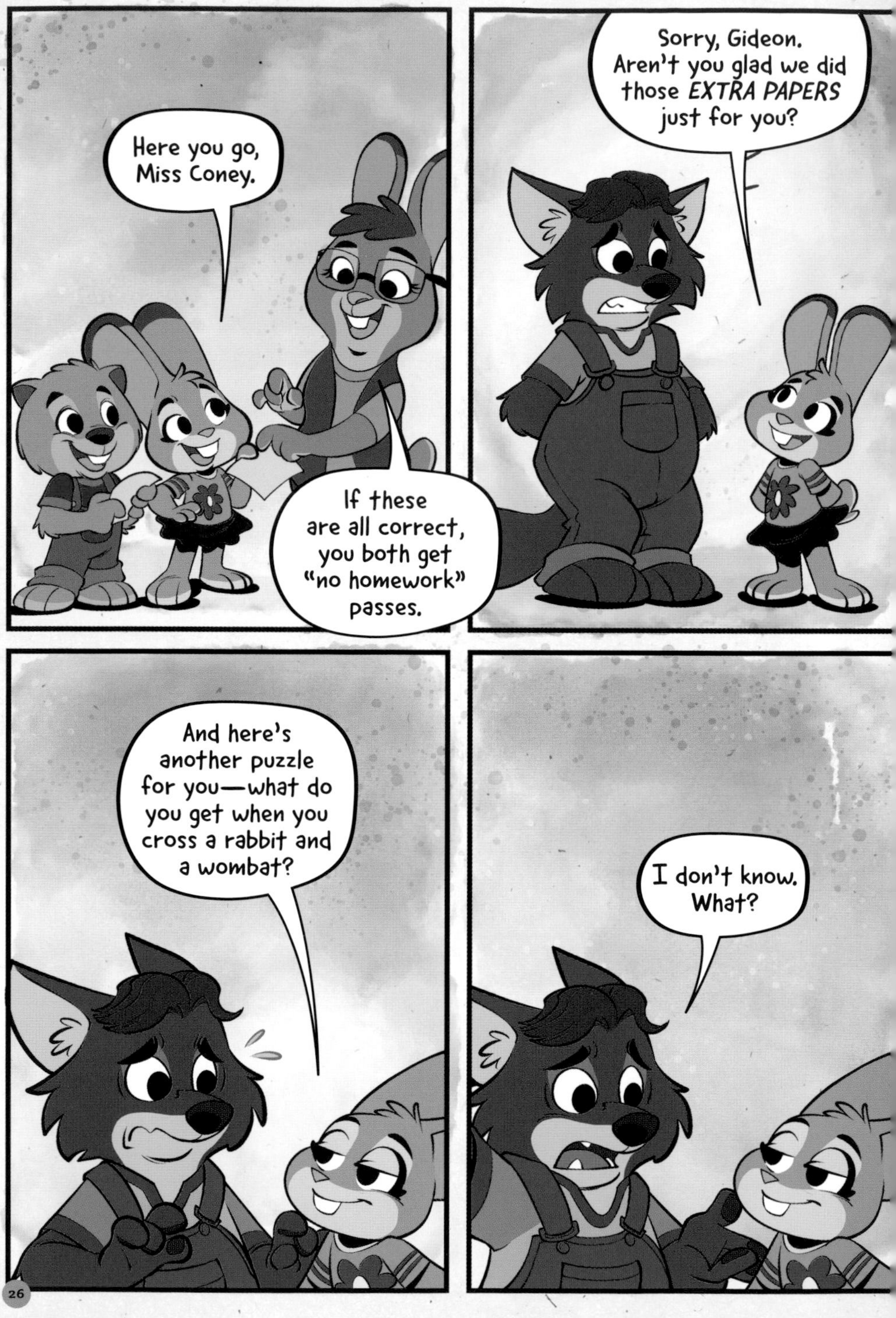
Here you go, Miss Coney.
If these are all correct, you both get "no homework" passes.
Sorry, Gideon. Aren't you glad we did those EXTRA PAPERS just for you?
And here's another puzzle for you—what do you get when you cross a rabbit and a wombat?
I don't know. What?

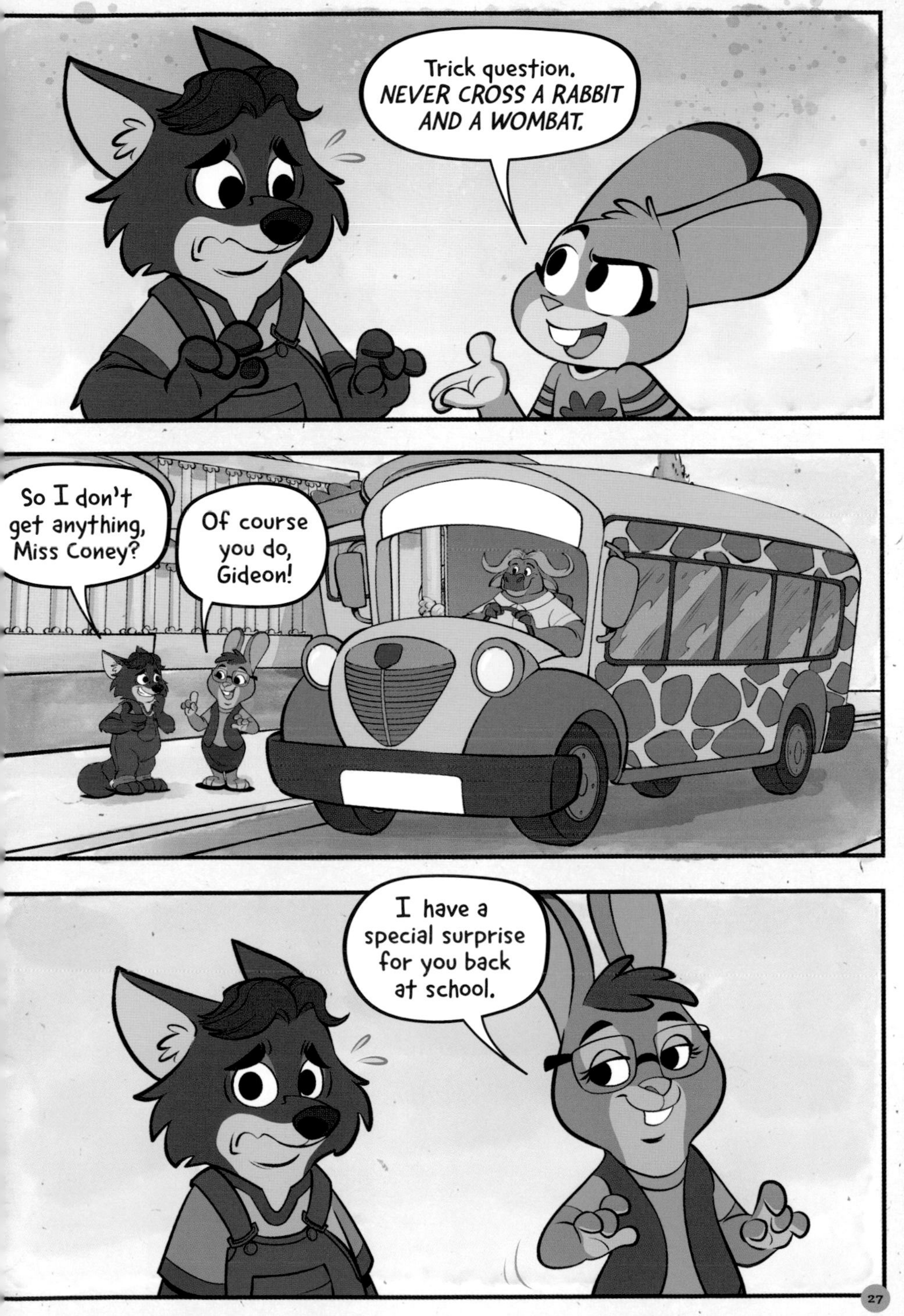
Trick question. NEVER CROSS A RABBIT AND A WOMBAT.
So I don't get anything, Miss Coney?
Of course you do, Gideon!
I have a special surprise for you back at school.

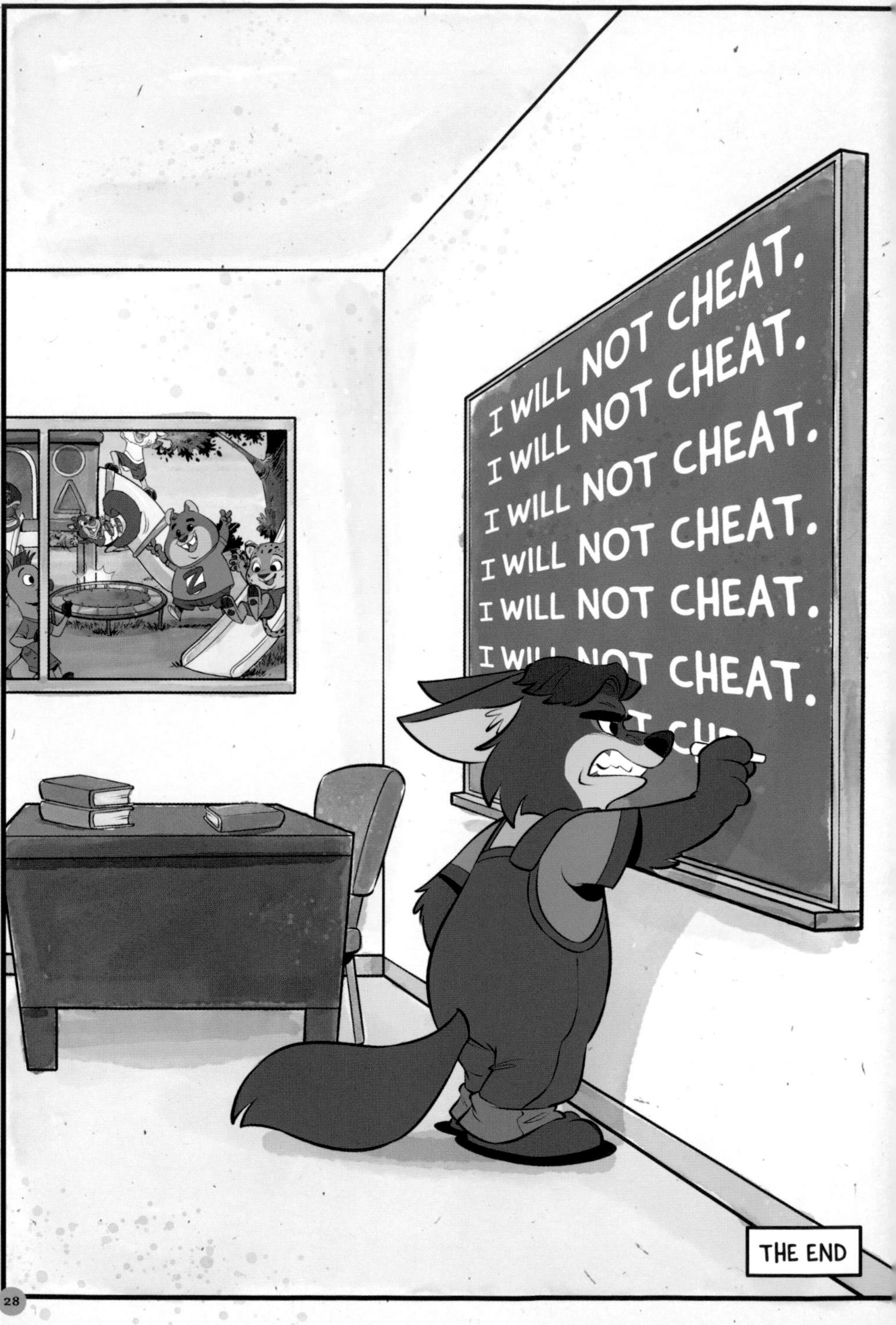
I WILL NOT CHEAT.
I WILL NOT CHEAT.
I WILL NOT CHEAT.
I WILL NOT CHEAT.
I WILL NOT CHEAT.
T CHEAT.
THE END

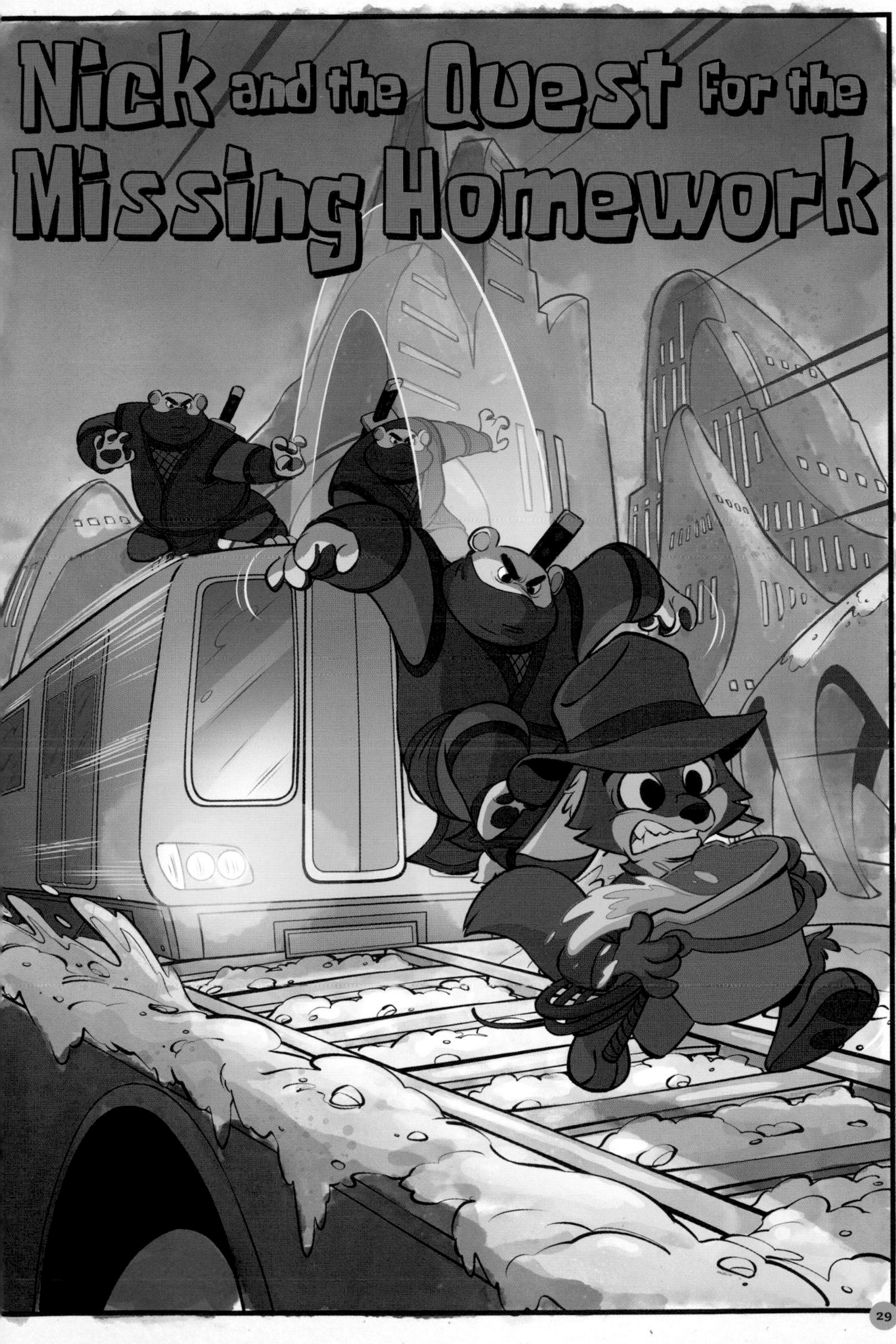
Nick and the Quest for the Missing Homework

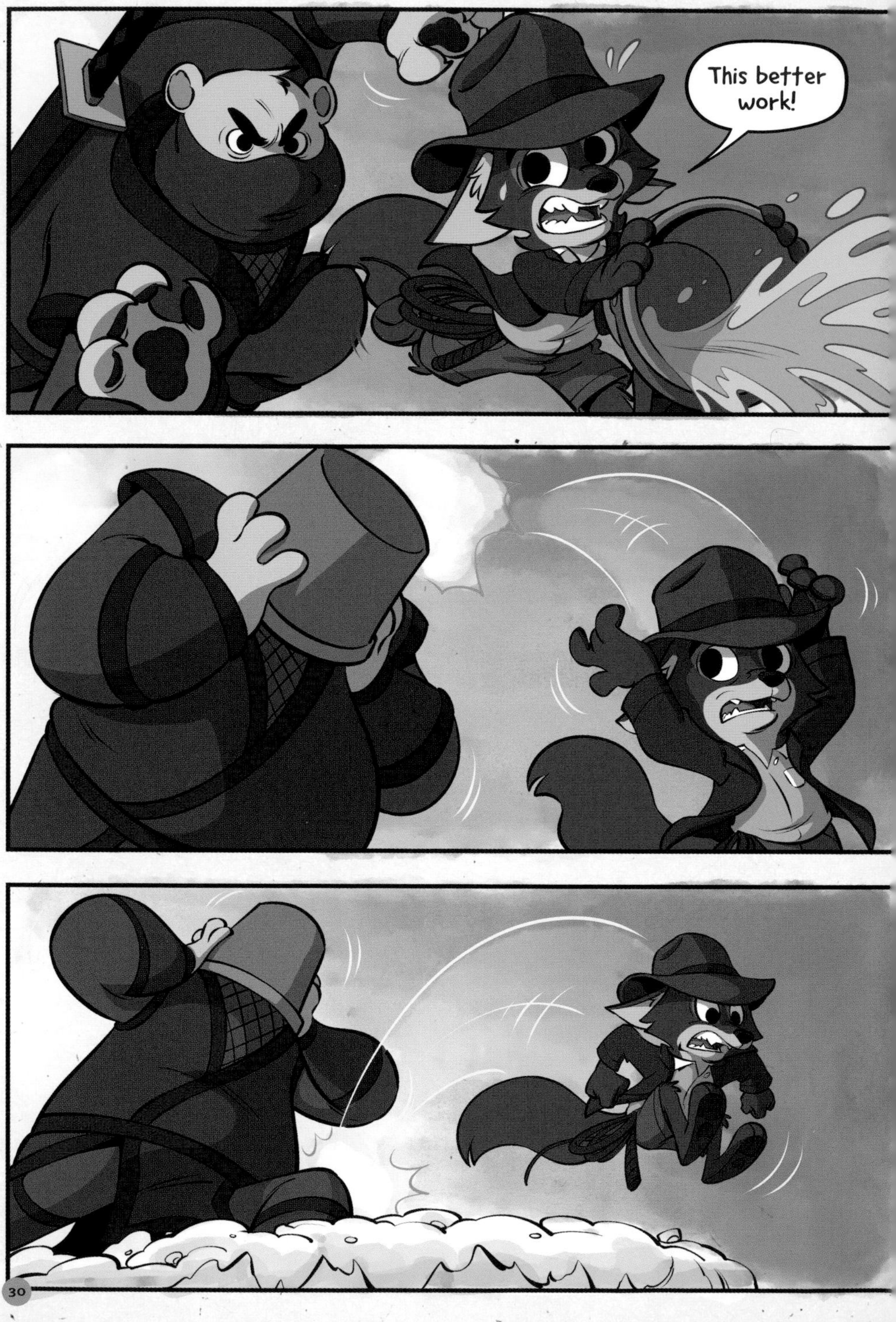
This better work!

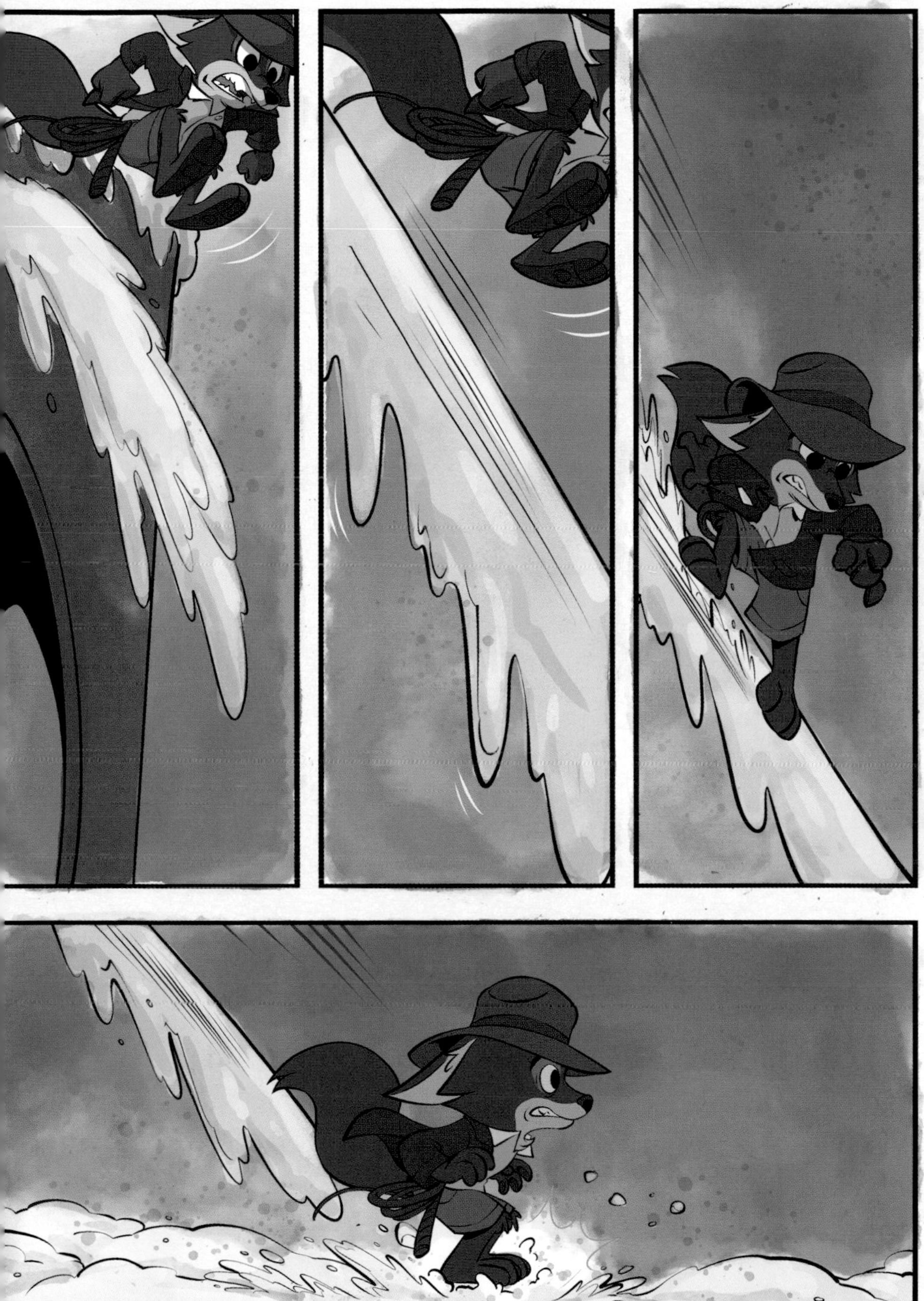

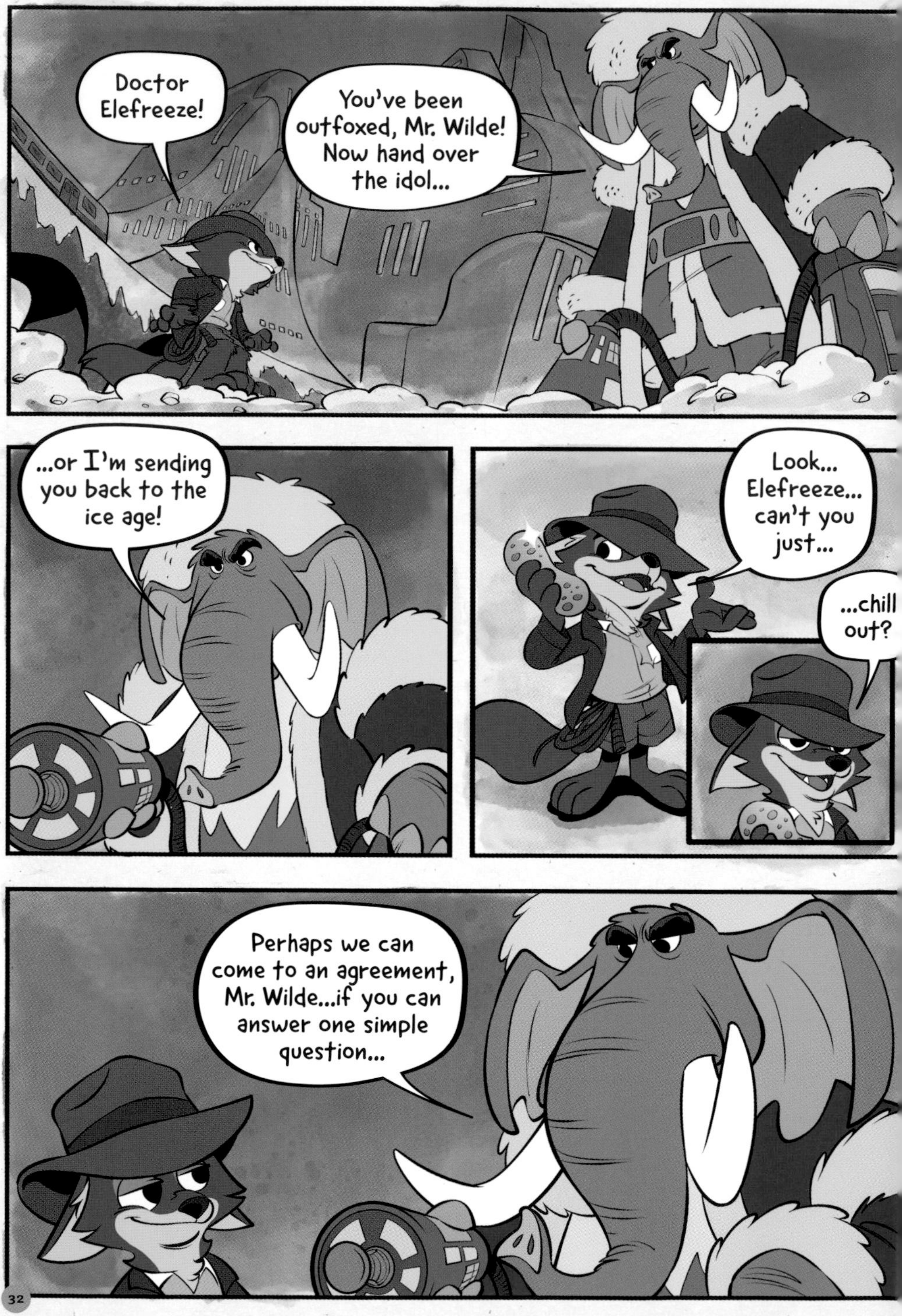
Doctor Elefreeze!
You've been outfoxed, Mr. Wilde! Now hand over the idol...
...or I'm sending you back to the ice age!
Look... Elefreeze... can't you just...
...chill out?
Perhaps we can come to an agreement, Mr. Wilde...if you can answer one simple question...

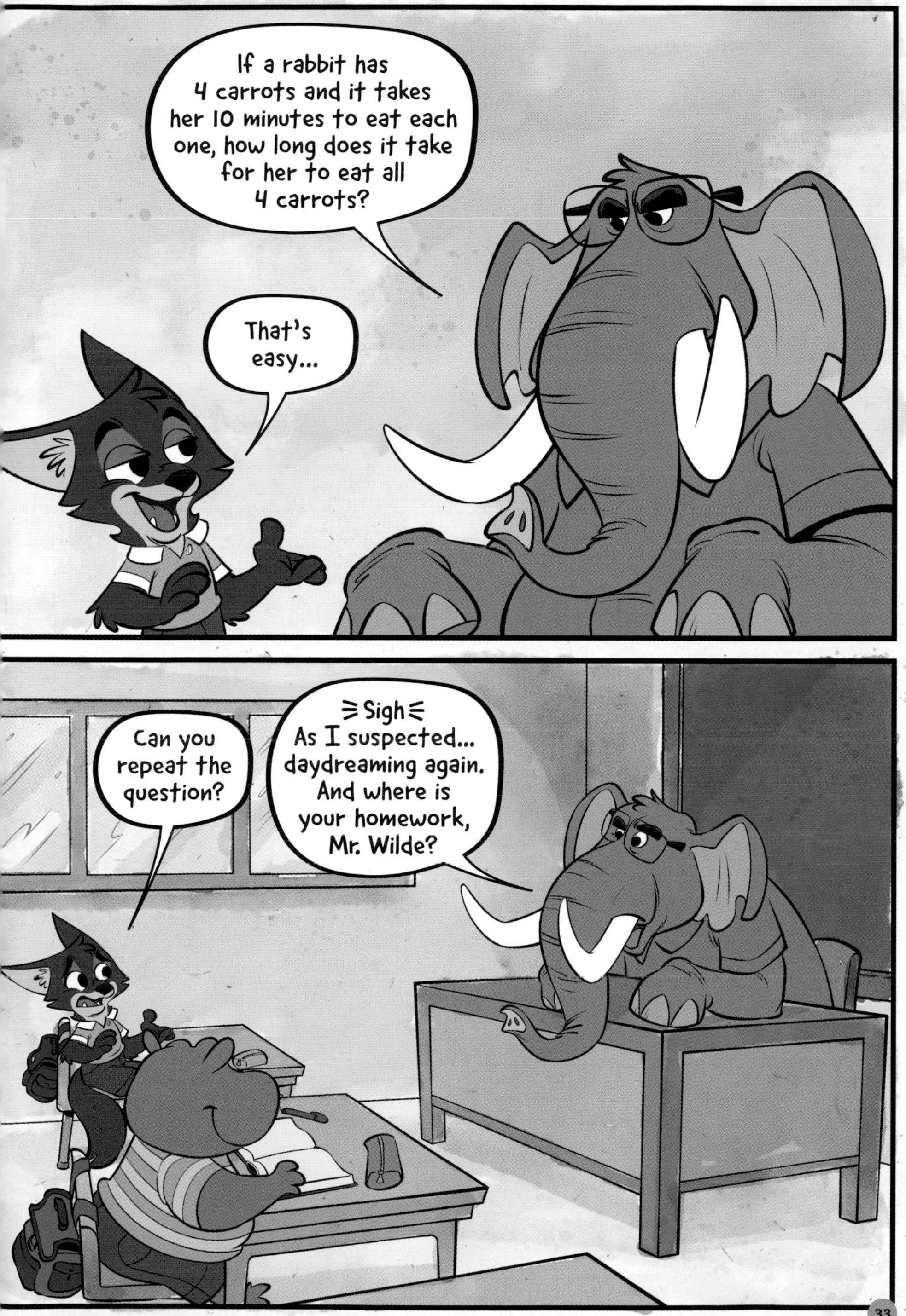
If a rabbit has 4 carrots and it takes her 10 minutes to eat each one, how long does it take for her to eat all 4 carrots?
That's easy...
Can you repeat the question?
⚞Sigh⚟ As I suspected... daydreaming again. And where is your homework, Mr. Wilde?

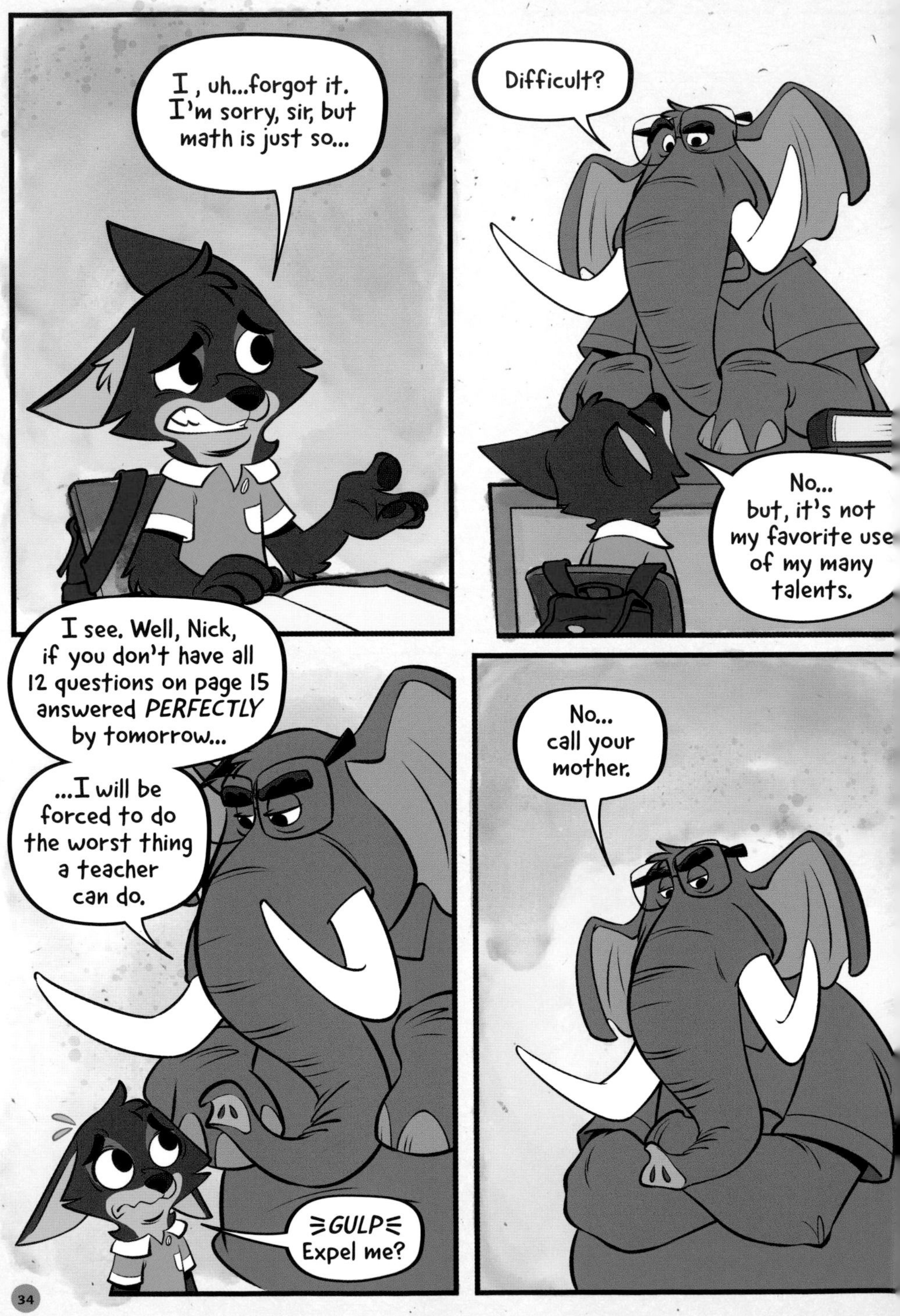
I, uh...forgot it. I'm sorry, sir, but math is just so...
Difficult?
No... but, it's not my favorite use of my many talents.
I see. Well, Nick, if you don't have all 12 questions on page 15 answered *PERFECTLY* by tomorrow...
...I will be forced to do the worst thing a teacher can do.
GULP
Expel me?
No... call your mother.

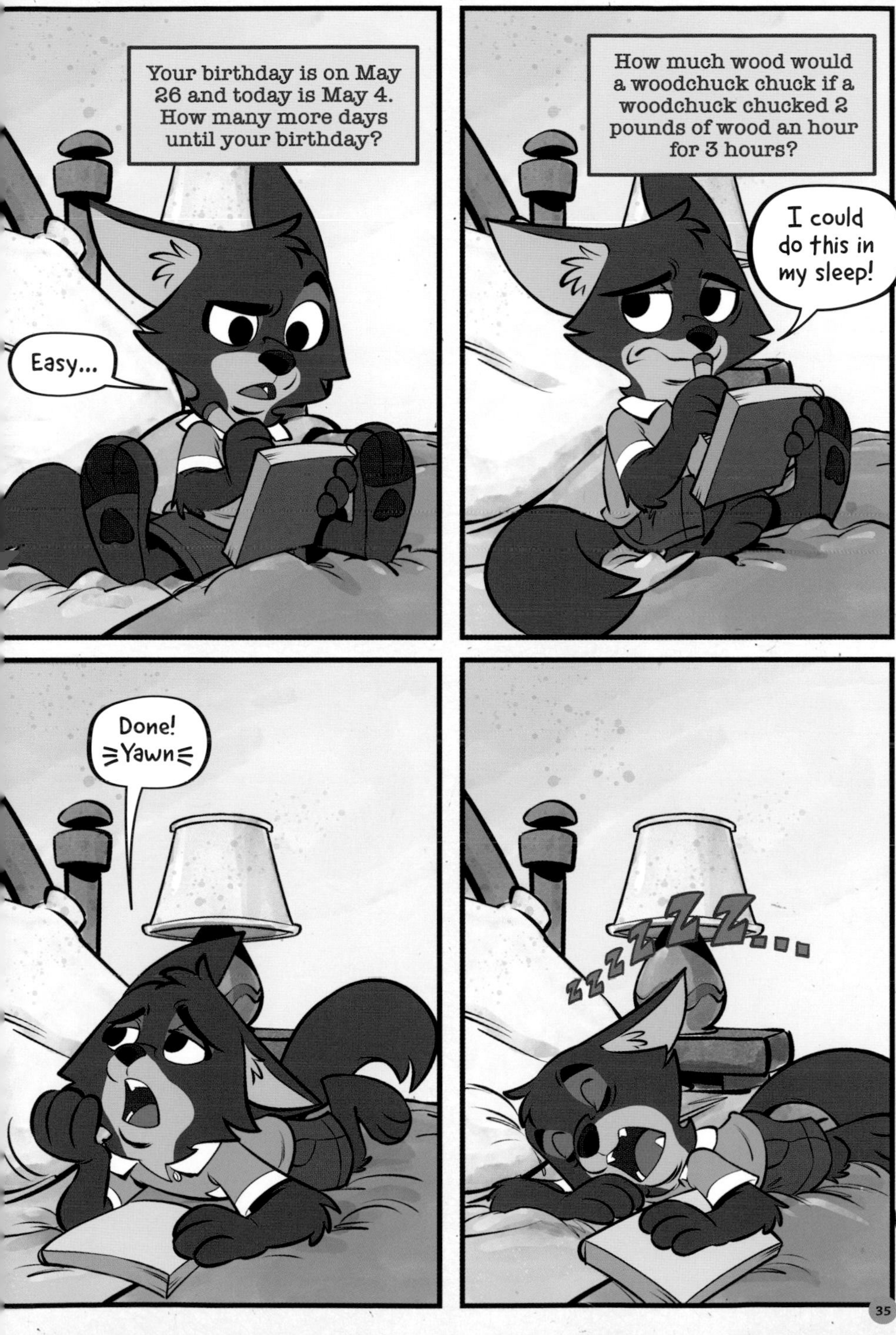
Your birthday is on May 26 and today is May 4. How many more days until your birthday?
Easy...
How much wood would a woodchuck chuck if a woodchuck chucked 2 pounds of wood an hour for 3 hours?
I could do this in my sleep!
Done!
Yawn
ZZZZZZZ...

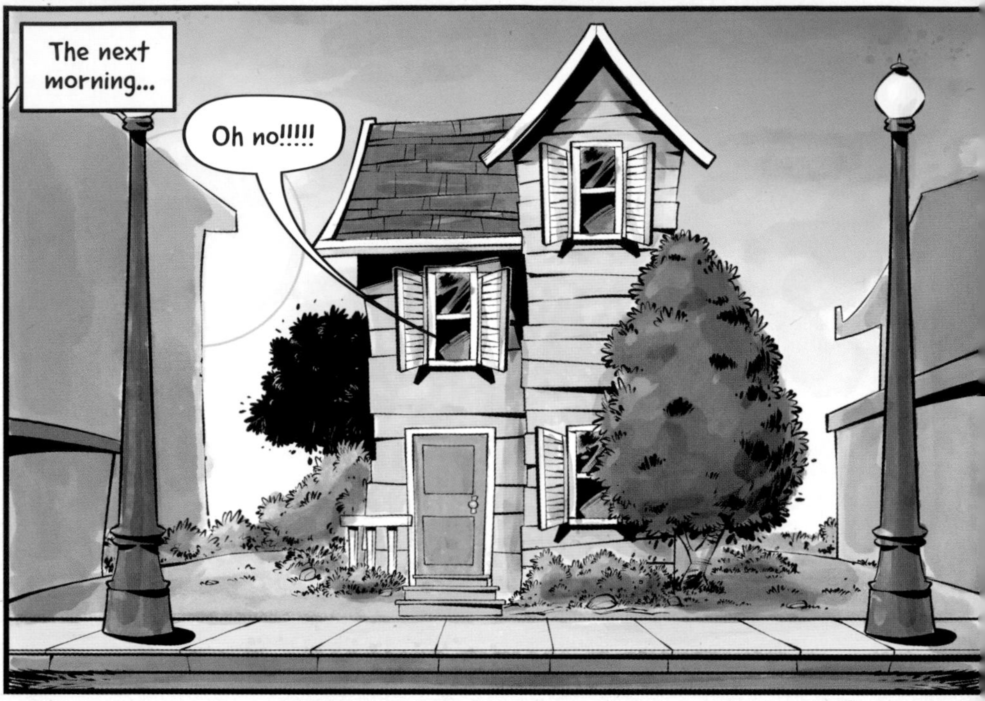
The next morning...
Oh no!!!!!

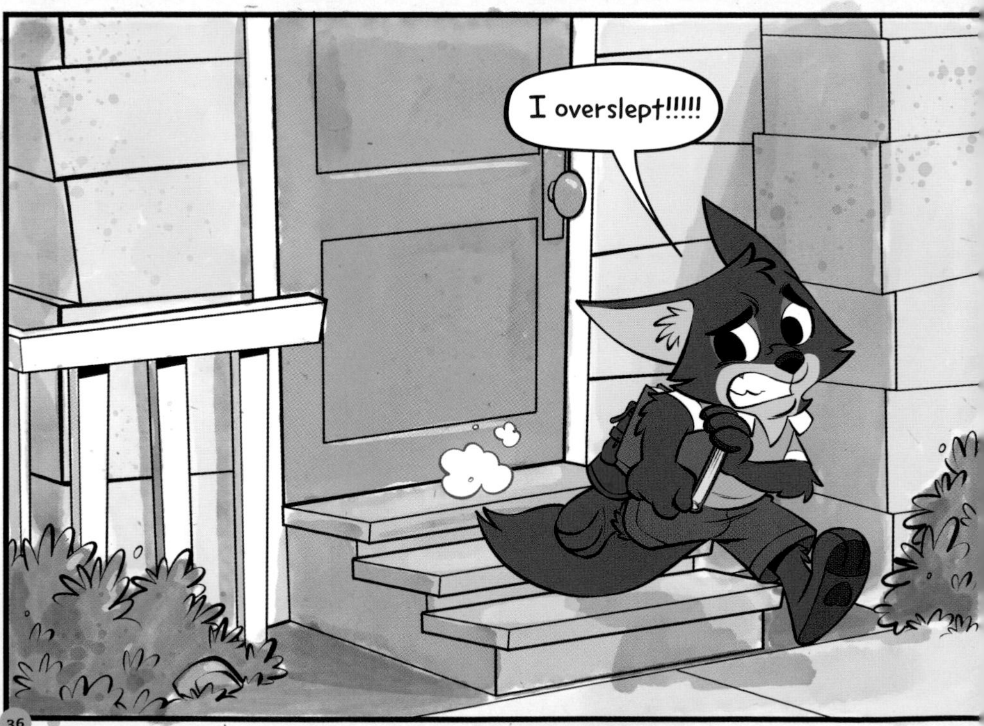
I overslept!!!!!

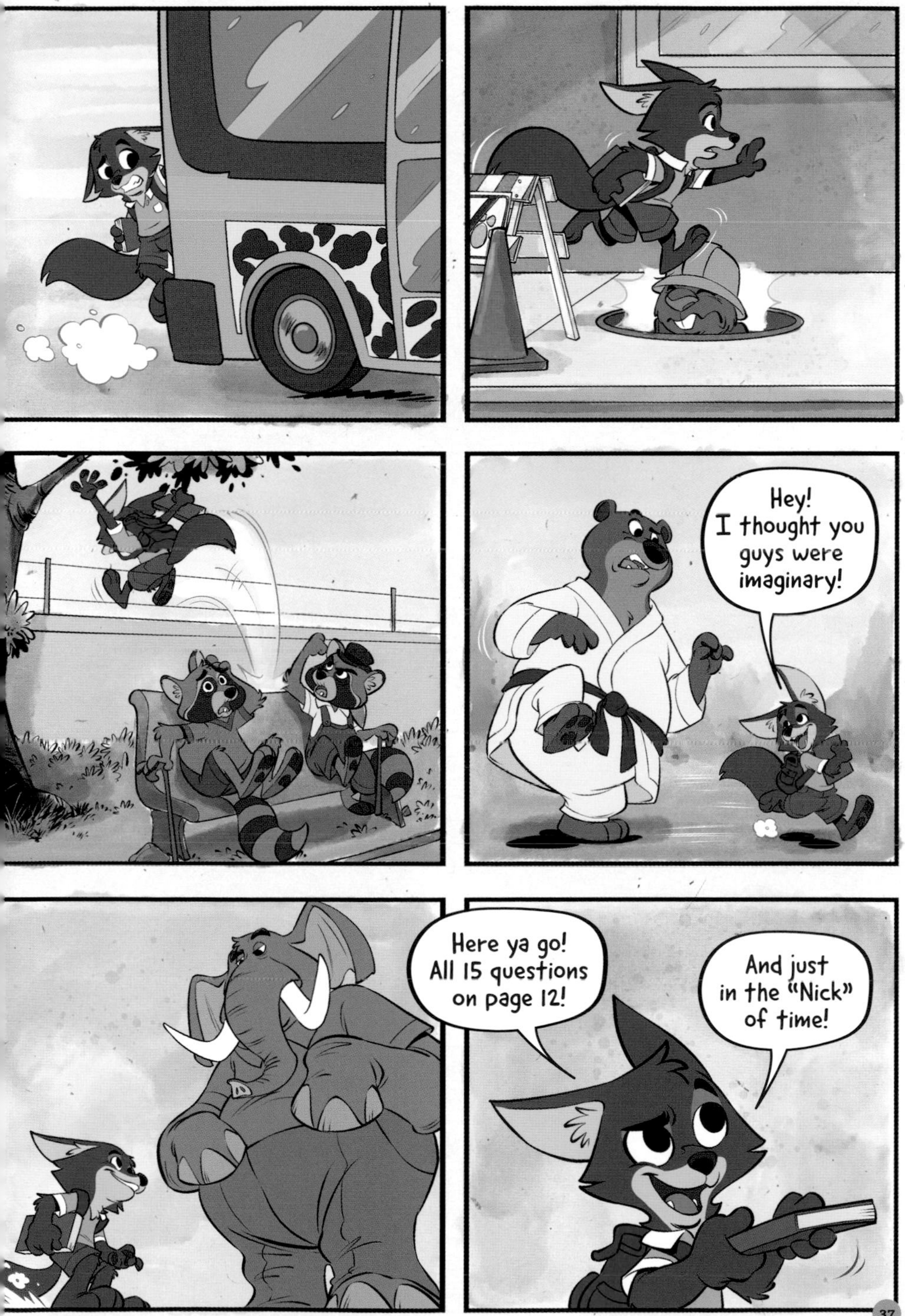
Hey!
I thought you
guys were
imaginary!
Here ya go!
All 15 questions
on page 12!
And just
in the "Nick"
of time!

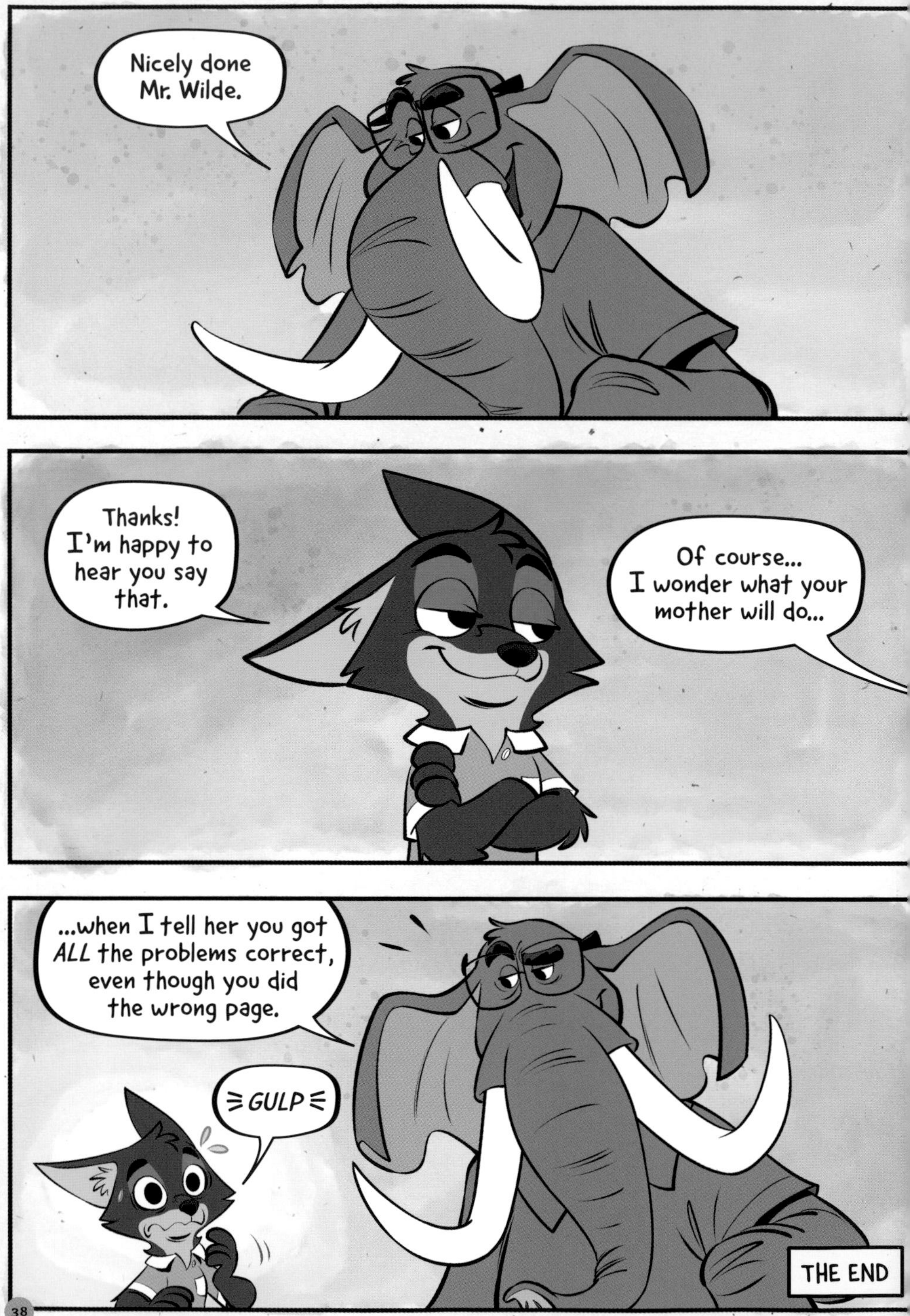
Nicely done Mr. Wilde.
Thanks! I'm happy to hear you say that.
Of course... I wonder what your mother will do...
...when I tell her you got *ALL* the problems correct, even though you did the wrong page.
GULP
THE END

FUN ACTIVITIES TO INSPIRE AND AMUSE!

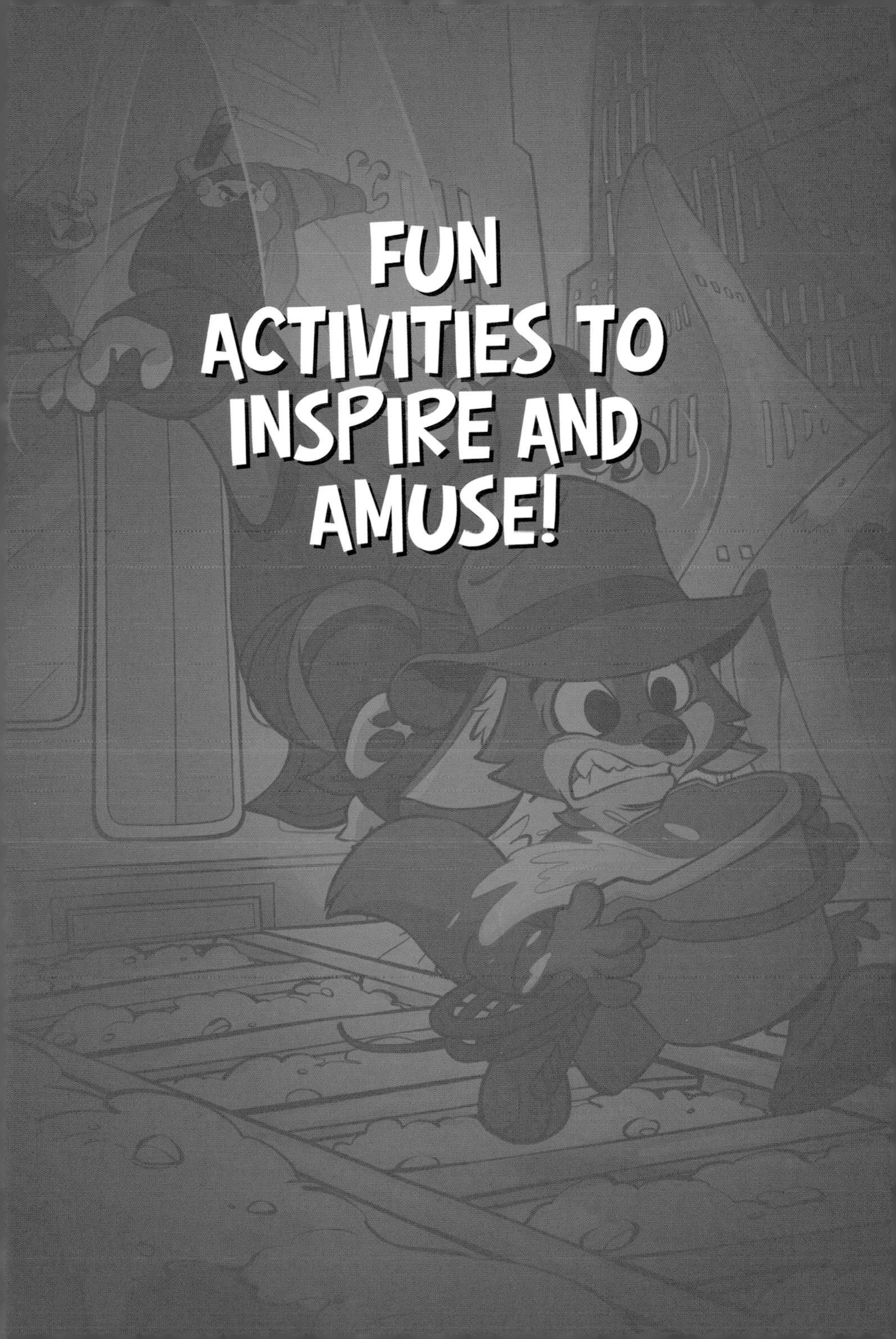

WHAT'S MISSING F

LOOK AT THE TWO PICTURES ON THESE PAGES OF JUDY, HER CLASSMATES, AND MISS CONEY AT THE MUSEUM. IT'S THE SAME PICTURE . . . OR IS IT? CAN YOU SPOT 10 DIFFERENCES BETWEEN PICTURE A, AND PICTURE B? THERE ARE SOME THINGS MISSING!

A

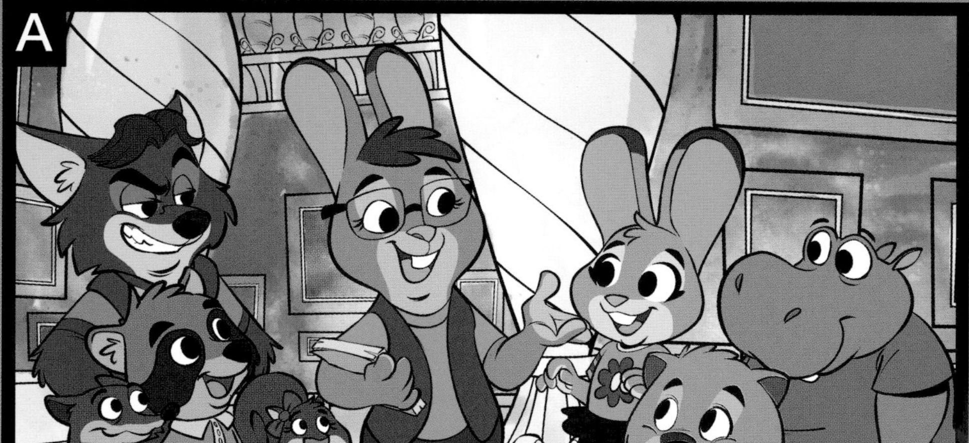

OM THE PICTURE?

WHEN YOU THINK YOU'VE FOUND ALL THE DIFFERENCES YOU CAN CHECK YOUR ANSWERS AT THE BOTTOM OF PAGE 43!

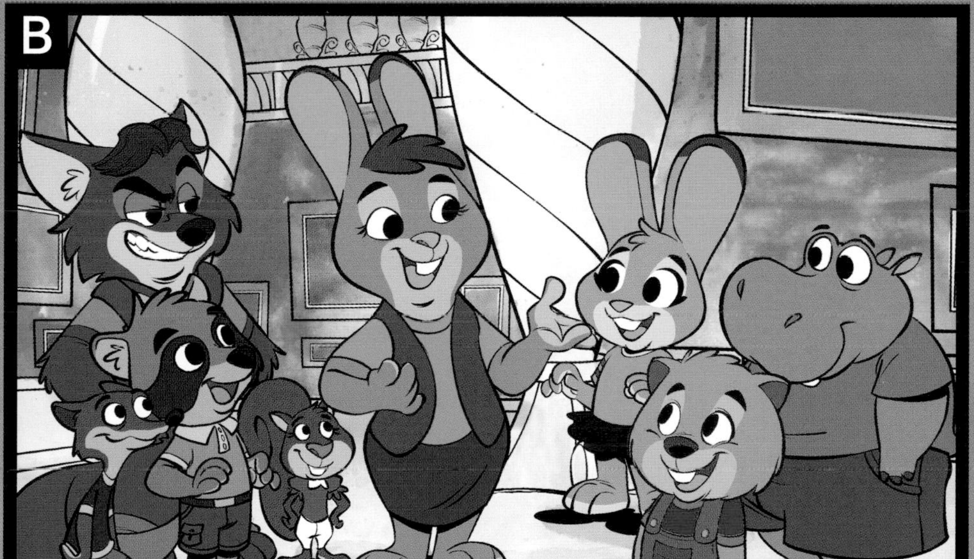
B

SCAVENGER HUNT!

CAN YOU FIND THESE ITEMS IN THE "THE MUSEUM LESSON" STORY?

❶ grey mouse

❷ straw hat

❸ pink book

❹ blue flag

❺ gearshift

CAN YOU FIND THESE ITEMS IN THE "NICK AND THE QUEST FOR THE MISSING HOMEWORK" STORY?

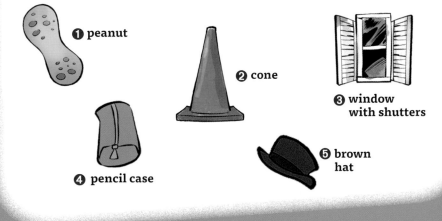

❶ peanut

❷ cone

❸ window with shutters

❹ pencil case

❺ brown hat

Scavenger Hunt answer key:
"Nick and the Quest for the Missing Homework": peanut, page 4; cone, page 9; window with shutters, page 8; pencil case, page 5; brown hat, page 9

Scavenger Hunt answer key:
"The Museum Lesson": grey mouse, page 7; straw hat, page 16; pink book, page 22; blue flag, page 1; gearshift, page 3

WHO AM I?

**For this activity, you'll need a partner

IMAGINE YOURSELF AS ONE OF THE CHARACTERS FROM "THE MUSEUM LESSON" STORY, SHOWN BELOW—BUT KEEP IT A SECRET FROM YOUR PARTNER BECAUSE THEY ARE GOING TO TRY TO GUESS WHO YOU ARE!

JUDY
she is a bunny

WILL
he is a wombat

GIDEON
he is a fox

MISS CONEY
she is a rabbit

Once you've decided who you are going to be, your partner can start asking you questions about yourself, until they can guess who you are. But, here's the hard part: you can only answer questions with "yes," "no," or "I don't know." **Below are a few examples of questions your partner might ask you!**

- Do you have sharp teeth?
- Do you have a long tail?
- Do you have big ears?
- Do you wear glasses?
- Are you an herbivore?

Once your partner has successfully guessed who you are, swap roles! Have your partner pick one of the characters and you ask the questions.

For an extra challenge, try this activity with one of the many different characters from "The Museum Lesson" story—there are lots of other students on the field trip!

What's Missing from the Picture answer key:

WHAT'S MISSING FROM THE PICTURE?

LOOK AT THE TWO PICTURES ON THESE PAGES OF NICK IN HIS DAYDREAM HAVING A SHOWDOWN WITH ELEFREEZE. IT'S THE SAME PICTURE . . . OR IS IT? CAN YOU SPOT 10 DIFFERENCES BETWEEN PICTURE A, AND PICTURE B? THERE ARE SOME THINGS MISSING!

WHEN YOU THINK YOU'VE FOUND ALL THE DIFFERENCES YOU CAN CHECK YOUR ANSWERS AT THE BOTTOM OF PAGE 46!

A

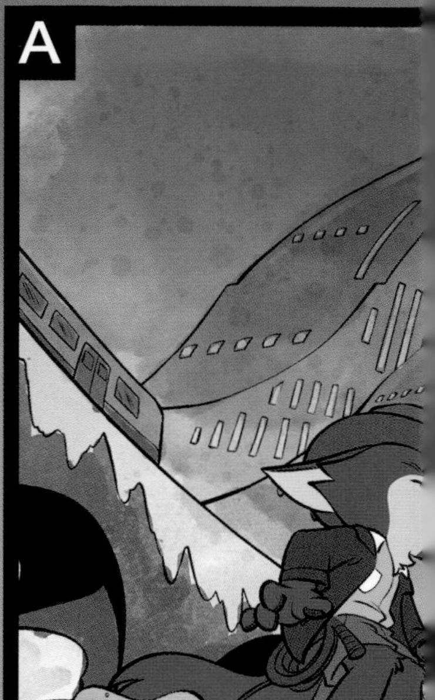

B

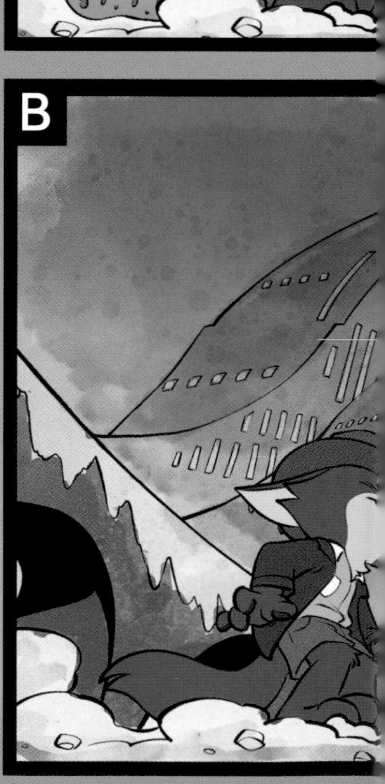

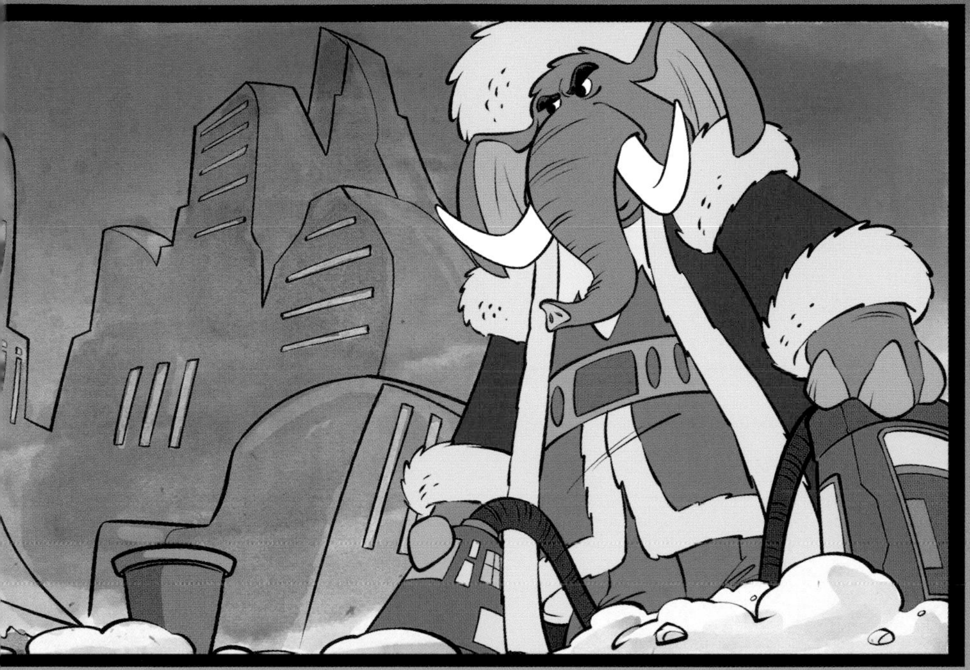

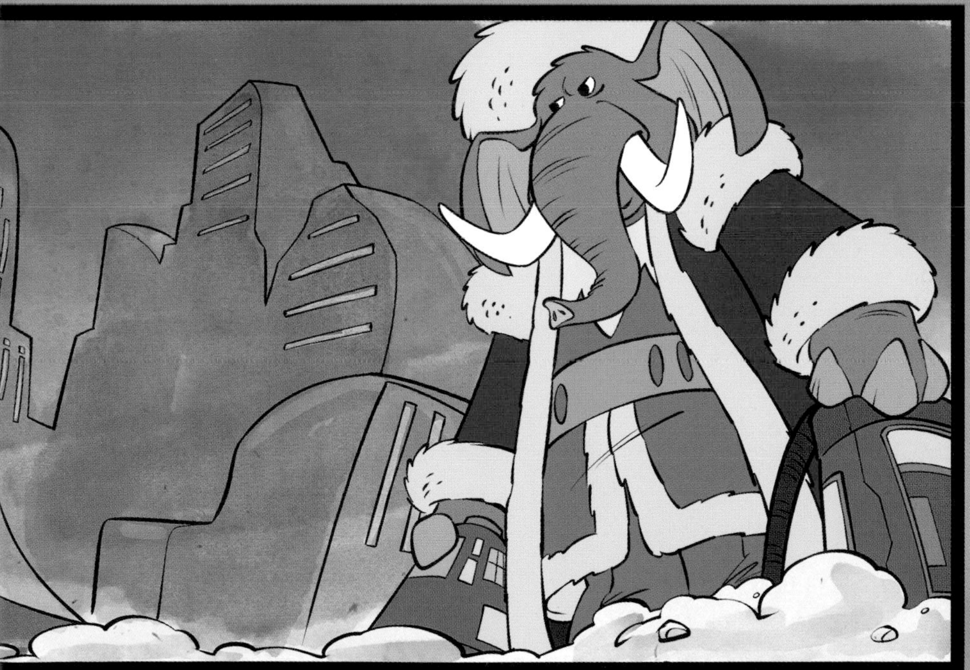

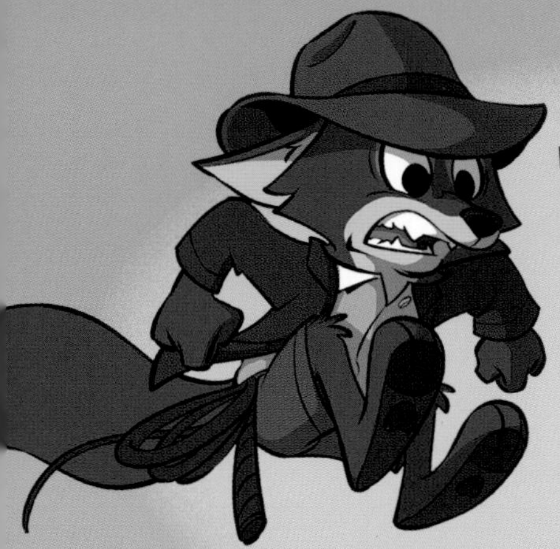

TONGUE TWISTER!

LET'S PLAY A GAME OF TONGUE TWISTERS! A TONGUE TWISTER IS A SEQUENCE OF WORDS THAT IS CHALLENGING TO PRONOUNCE QUICKLY AND ACCURATELY. THEY ARE A FUN WAY TO PRACTICE AND IMPROVE PRONUNCIATION!

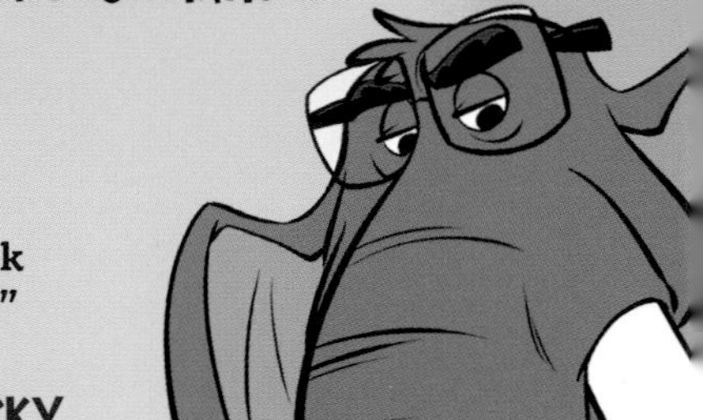

For example, in Nick's story, Nick reads a question in his homework assignment that begins with a tongue twister:

"How much wood would a woodchuck chuck if a woodchuck chucked 2 pounds of wood?"

CAN YOU ENUNCIATE? HERE ARE EIGHT TRICKY TONGUE TWISTERS TO TRY TO TIE YOUR TONGUE:

- **Slithery sliding snails slowly slip the surface.**
- **Reading and writing are really richly rewarding.**
- **Five nice mice make merry music by moonlight.**
- **I scream, you scream, we all scream for ice cream.**
- **Around the rugged rocks the rushing rabbits run.**
- **Lazy lizards lick lunch while lying on lilypads.**
- **Green grassy groves give great grub to goats.**
- **Light nights like tonight need no night lights.**

With each of the tongue twisting sentences above, challenge yourself to see how fast you can clearly say each one. Pick one and try saying it three times as fast as you can. If that feels easy, try saying it five times—even faster.

Try out all the tongue twisters to see how tired your tongue can get. If you have a friend nearby, you could take turns!

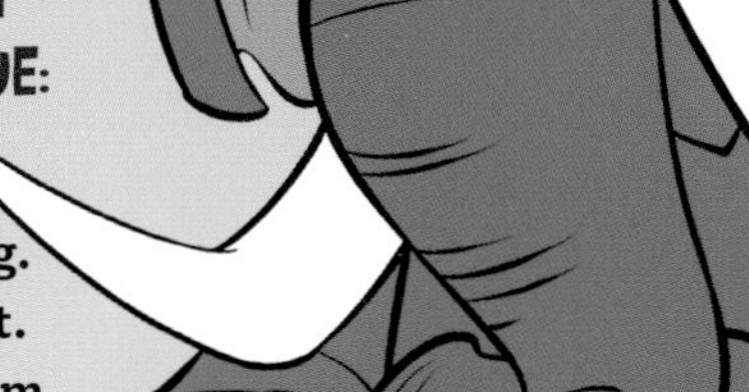
What's Missing from the Picture answer key:

DARK HORSE BOOKS

president and publisher Mike Richardson • collection editor Freddye Miller • collection assistant editor Judy Khuu • collection designer David Nestelle • digital art technician Christianne Gillenardo-Goudreau

Neil Hankerson Executive Vice President • Tom Weddle Chief Financial Officer • Randy Stradley Vice President of Publishing • Nick McWhorter Chief Business Development Officer • Dale LaFountain Chief Information Officer • Matt Parkinson Vice President of Marketing • Cara Niece Vice President of Production and Scheduling • Mark Bernardi Vice President of Book Trade and Digital Sales • Ken Lizzi General Counsel • Dave Marshall Editor in Chief • Davey Estrada Editorial Director • Chris Warner Senior Books Editor • Cary Grazzini Director of Specialty Projects • Lia Ribacchi Art Director • Vanessa Todd-Holmes Director of Print Purchasing • Matt Dryer Director of Digital Art and Prepress • Michael Gombos Senior Director of Licensed Publications • Kari Yadro Director of Custom Programs • Kari Torson Director of International Licensing • Sean Brice Director of Trade Sales

DISNEY PUBLISHING WORLDWIDE GLOBAL MAGAZINES, COMICS AND PARTWORKS

PUBLISHER Lynn Waggoner • EDITORIAL TEAM Bianca Coletti (Director, Magazines), Guido Frazzini (Director, Comics), Carlotta Quattrocolo (Executive Editor), Stefano Ambrosio (Executive Editor, New IP), Camilla Vedove (Senior Manager, Editorial Development), Behnoosh Khalili (Senior Editor), Julie Dorris (Senior Editor), Mina Riazi (Assistant Editor) • DESIGN Enrico Soave (Senior Designer) • ART Ken Shue (VP, Global Art), Manny Mederos (Senior Illustration Manager, Comics and Magazines), Roberto Santillo (Creative Director), Marco Ghiglione (Creative Manager), Stefano Attardi (Illustration Manager) • PORTFOLIO MANAGEMENT Olivia Ciancarelli (Director) • BUSINESS & MARKETING Mariantonietta Galla (Senior Manager, Franchise), Virpi Korhonen (Editorial Manager)

Zootopia: School Days

Published by Dark Horse Books
A division of Dark Horse Comics LLC
10956 SE Main Street
Milwaukie, OR 97222

DarkHorse.com

To find a comics shop in your area, visit comicshoplocator.com

First edition: October 2019
ISBN 978-1-50671-205-5
Digital ISBN 978-1-50671-207-9

1 3 5 7 9 10 8 6 4 2
Printed in China

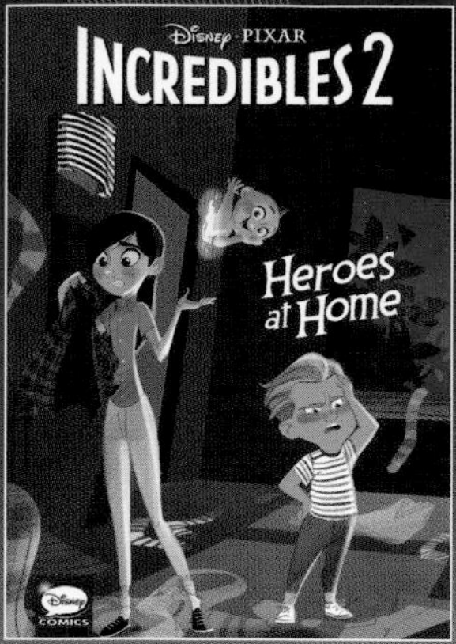
Disney·PIXAR
INCREDIBLES 2
Heroes at Home
Disney COMICS

LOOKING FOR BOOKS FOR YOUNGER READERS?

$7.99 each!

EACH VOLUME INCLUDES A SECTION OF FUN ACTIVITIES!

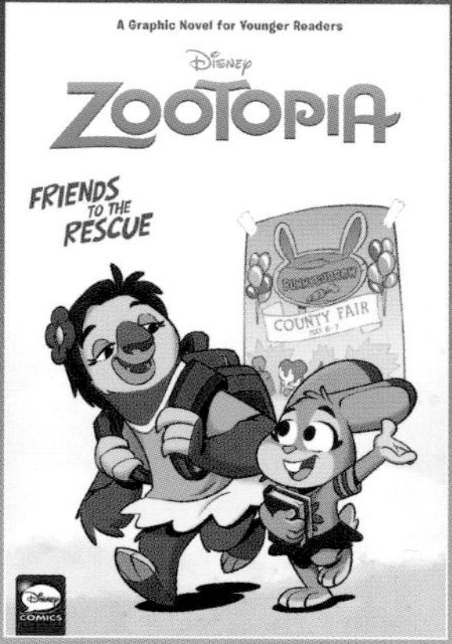
A Graphic Novel for Younger Readers
Disney
ZOOTOPIA
FRIENDS TO THE RESCUE
COUNTY FAIR
Disney COMICS

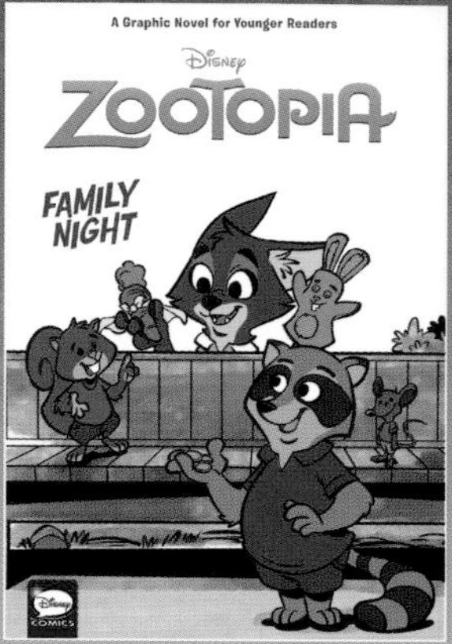
A Graphic Novel for Younger Readers
Disney
ZOOTOPIA
FAMILY NIGHT
Disney COMICS

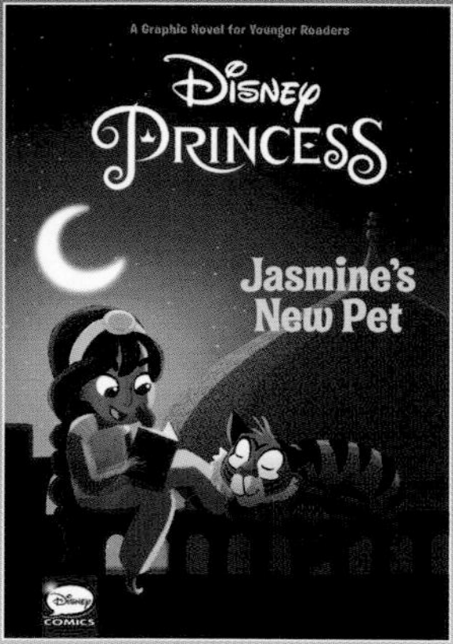
A Graphic Novel for Younger Readers
Disney
PRINCESS
Jasmine's New Pet
Disney COMICS

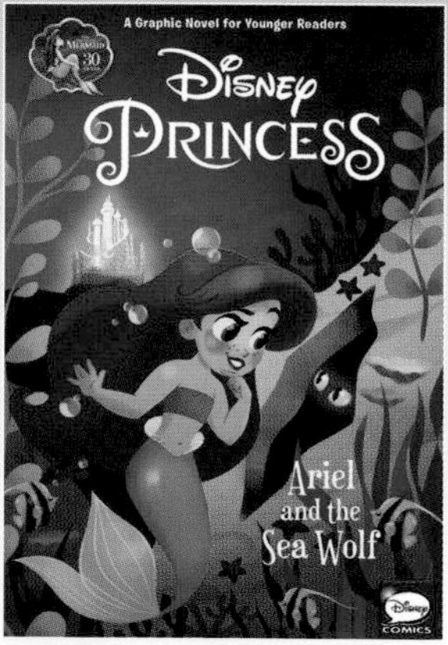
A Graphic Novel for Younger Readers
Disney
PRINCESS
Ariel and the Sea Wolf
Disney COMICS

DISNEY ZOOTOPIA: FRIENDS TO THE RESCUE
ISBN 978-1-50671-054-9
DISNEY ZOOTOPIA: FAMILY NIGHT
ISBN 978-1-50671-053-2
Join young Judy Hopps as she uses wit and bravery to solve mysteries, conundrums, and more! And quick-thinking young Nick Wilde won't be stopped from achieving his goals—where there's a will, there's a way!

DISNEY·PIXAR INCREDIBLES 2: HEROES AT HOME
ISBN 978-1-50670-943-7
Being part of a Super family means helping out at home, too. Can Violet and Dash pick up groceries and secretly stop some bad guys? And can they clean up the house while Jack-Jack is "sleeping"?

DISNEY PRINCESS: JASMINE'S NEW PET
ISBN 978-1-50671-052-5
Jasmine has a new pet tiger, Rajah, but he's not quite ready for palace life. Will she be able to train the young cub before the Sultan finds him another home?

DISNEY PRINCESS: ARIEL AND THE SEA WOLF
ISBN 978-1-50671-203-1
Ariel accidentally drops a bracelet into a cave that supposedly contains a dangerous creature. Her curiosity implores her to enter, and what she finds turns her quest for a bracelet into a quest for truth.

AVAILABLE AT YOUR LOCAL COMICS SHOP OR BOOKSTORE! TO FIND A COMICS SHOP IN YOUR AREA, VISIT COMICSHOPLOCATOR.COM

DARK HORSE BOOKS

For more information or to order direct: On the web: DarkHorse.com | Email: mailorder@darkhorse.com | Phone: 1-800-862-0052 Mon.–Fri. 9 a.m. to 5 p.m. Pacific Time

DISNEY COMICS